AFTERNOONS IN PARIS

AFTERNOONS IN PARIS

A Francis Bacon Mystery

JANICE LAW

MYSTERIOUSPRESS.COM

INTEGRATED MEDIA

NEW YORK

Copyright © 2017 by Janice Law

Cover design by Mauricio Díaz

978-1-5040-3641-2

Published in 2017 by MysteriousPress.com/Open Road Integrated Media, Inc.
180 Maiden Lane
New York, NY 10038
www.mysteriouspress.com
www.openroadmedia.com

For Anne Galloway

AFTERNOONS IN PARIS

CHAPTER ONE

"Just sneaky-weaky over here and hold this, Francis," Armand said. Of course, he said it in French because he speaks no English except *Hello, Francis*, which was how he greeted me when I arrived at the studio in the morning—and if I had stayed over and gotten up early, which I always did, to make a pot of coffee first thing. *Hello, Francis*, he would say and pat me on the bum and giggle, because he was a right old queen. But nice, I had to say, nice, and, as I'd written more than once to Nan, an excellent teacher.

What was I learning in the City of Light, the Art Capital of the World? A multitude of things, and much more pleasantly, if less excitingly, than in Berlin. My *français* was improving by leaps and bounds, although much of it, like my German, was not fit for polite company. This amused Armand, who was affected and fastidious but not as timid as he liked to pretend. He would tell me I was shocking and fan himself, and then he'd get a gleam in his eye and get me to drop whatever work I was doing to help him with his hobby and his passion, his "art" photography.

His real work was designing rugs, fabrics, wallpapers, and the occasional furniture piece, along with screens and various high-end decorations. His work was very skillful, if not as innovative as the Bauhaus pieces I saw in Berlin. Armand leaned toward art deco, and his fabric designs, full of sinuous flowers and leaves, looked back toward art nouveau.

I was becoming familiar with them because Armand was lazy. He sketched out the motifs and indicated the colors before he had me work up several repeats in gouache so clients could see the effects in fabric or wallpaper. If a design was approved, he'd set me to doing anywhere from two to five color variations. It was careful, tedious work, but I was learning a great deal about color harmonies and contrasting shapes.

Because Armand was generous with both praise and criticism, I was becoming technically skillful. Just yesterday, I was working on a version of a tulip pattern in blues and browns, impossible for the flowers but a favorite harmony among fashionable decorators. "*Le marché,* Francis, *le marché, c'est le Dieu,*" Armand said, and then he looked at my work a long time with a thoughtful expression. "*Trés intéressant,*" he said. "But you must not add too many tones. Too expensive for this client. But good. You have a feel for these colors."

In my next letter to Nan, I'd be able to assure her that I was making progress, that blues and browns were my colors, that I'd been entrusted with making a first sketch for a rug. All this gave me hope of realizing my ambition to make a home with Nan. Let it be soon! While things were not as bad as they were immediately after the war, jobs were scarce and my dear nanny had been reduced to a wretched position with an elderly invalid in

Brighton. She wrote me amusing letters about this gorgon, but I could tell she was unhappy.

When I was small, I often dreamed of living alone with Nan instead of with Nan and my disapproving and unsympathetic family. Now that I was old enough to make that wish come true, I intended to support us in London as a designer. And Armand was my ticket, because he understood the principles of design and how to work with manufacturers and how to present ideas to clients.

So when he asked me to *sneaky over* to the modeling stand, I washed off my brush and left the stylized iris I was painting unfinished. I moved Armand's lights around for him then waited to see what was to be the subject *du jour*. Sometimes he had a model, one of the pros, sturdy compact men with well-defined muscles and the strength to hold long and difficult poses in the ateliers. Or one of the *garçons* off the street, thin and hungry and sometimes larcenous.

But today, the subject was *moi*. I would rather be painting. Armand was fine; I didn't at all mind going to bed with him. It was the elaborate preliminaries that got me down, because *le maître* required elaborate little dramas. Perhaps I could tell Nan that I was learning the theatrical trade as well.

Armand put his arms in the air and lifted one foot. "*Le danseur*," he said.

One of our favorites, a little glimpse of Bacchic revels— wouldn't my old classics master be impressed! In this one, I was a celebrant with a wreath of fake ivy around my brow and a strategic trailing scarf so that Armand could send some images to a respectable gallery. Some. The others were frankly pornographic and were kept for his private amusement.

He demonstrated each pose for me. I had to keep from giggling, because Armand, as fat as a prosperous butcher, was a most unlikely dancer. And yet he had something I did not: a feel for music, a sense of motion. I tried to repeat the gestures but failed, so that he had to step up on the stand and correct my position. This was par for the course, and half the time we didn't get any pictures at all but end up *en flagrante*, a new and useful term, on the modeling stand.

That was afternoons in the studio. All amusing in a way, but I still had another repeat of the tulips to paint, and if Armand was flirtatious, even kittenish, before, afterward he was all business. I was his apprentice, and while the master can knock off early and head out to a café, the apprentice needs to finish the piecework of the day.

"The client comes tomorrow, Francis!" he said, collecting his hat and his light jacket and sashaying off.

Of course, even late work was better than the alternative: imprisonment at some wretched school with Latin declensions or Greek verbs or other topics that would never pay the rent. Still, I hated missing Madame Dumoulin, my gallery-going acquaintance, who had planned to stop by Galerie Billiet this afternoon. Now I would surely be too late. Madame's tastes were catholic, and although a show of sculptures and toys made of wire sounded less interesting than paint on canvas, I learned something new every time I accompanied her.

We'd by chance met in the Palais de Luxembourg. I had just

finished cleaning the studio—the apprentice must keep things spick-and-span—and wandered in to see the famous Impressionists: bright skies, pretty women, and sporting types on an eternal holiday. Well, mostly. I did like Manet's *Olympia*, realistically skinny and cynical, lying naked on her bed while her *femme de chambre* brings her the most immense and beautiful bouquet and her black cat arches its back as if this visitor (or even *moi*, the spectator) is deeply unwelcome. I've been there and I can attest to the truth.

The Olympia, Victorine Meurent, was not only a famous model but a painter herself, and now I recognized her features in half a dozen canvases. I knew this thanks to Madame Dumoulin, who stopped next to one of Monet's *Nympheas* while I was looking at the huge canvas. Imagine a billboard in the most beautiful blues and greens imaginable, that's how big the painting seemed, and scattered across it were the water lilies, the botanical nymphs—more echoes of my classics master—with, and this is what interested me, no real center. The whole thing was like a beautiful length of fabric without a single repeat. I was standing there trying to figure out how it worked and what kept the eye from sliding off the canvas, when I became aware that someone was standing near me, also absorbed in the Monet.

She was tall with a fair, open face, strong features, and dark hair just beginning to be streaked with gray. She was wearing a simple taupe day dress with a jacket in a darker hue and a matching beret, an effortlessly elegant effect that was another mystery of French design. She smiled and, as if she had read my thoughts, said, "He has devised a new way of organizing the canvas. Am I right?"

It took me a minute to understand her comment—even

working for Armand, I had not had too many discussions about style or construction, his method being to give me a pattern and see that I copied it exactly. It took me a minute more to convey agreement in my weak French.

She began to point out some of the beauties of the canvas, and, when I indicated that I did not know all the French names of the colors, she repeated the shades carefully for me. She was, she told me, fascinated by Monet's experiments, by his late works, struggling as he was with cataracts. "How much art has been affected by failing vision," she remarked. "Degas, too."

I expressed my admiration for his portraits.

"And the dancers?"

"Marvelous," I said, "but I am interested in the human face." This surprised me a little as somehow I had not known that before. But, yes, if I ever painted, I would want to paint faces and bodies, not flowers or landscapes, no matter how beautiful. "Not exactly portraits," I added.

"Very wise," she said. "The photograph has ruined a lot of livelihoods. Shall we visit the Degases?"

I said, in the best French I could manage, I would be charmed, and she smiled. Without being beautiful or even pretty, she had a lovely face, a good smile. Though I am only interested in sex with men, I like women, especially clever older women who enjoy conversation and ideas.

"I am Madeline Dumoulin," she said, "and I visit the Degases as often as I can."

I told her my name and mentioned that I was working—studying, actually—with Monsieur Armand.

"*Formidable*," she said. We strolled through the galleries like old acquaintances, talking, despite my weak French, about every painting, every painter, the gallery light, the beauties of the gardens. Her charm made me miss Nan, who is full of eccentric and unconventional ideas and whose conversation is always interesting.

I did not really expect to meet Madame Dumoulin again, even though I looked in at the Luxembourg several times in the hope that I would. Then one day when I was window-shopping among the little galleries along the rue Bréa and rue de Grande Chaumière, I spotted her at L'Academie. She was wearing a pair of spectacles and examining a painting with the utmost concentration. I overcame my shyness and went inside. "*Bonjour*, Madame Dumoulin."

She turned and her face lit up. "*Monsieur Bacon! Quelle surprise!*"

As if we were continuing our previous conversation, she gestured toward the painting, a technically astonishing image of a woman as smoothly and firmly rendered as a motorcar. When I said this, Madame Dumoulin laughed, corrected my grammar, and laughed again.

"*Tres vrai!*" she said, and we spent a happy hour admiring and criticizing the work. As we were leaving, she remarked that Thursday was her day for Paris, that she spent all afternoon in one gallery or another and usually took in a concert or a play at night. From then on, I was sure to be around the museums or the galleries on Thursdays, and more often than not, I met Madame Dumoulin, who started to mention plans for seeing such and such a show or visiting certain galleries of the Louvre on her next visit. You could be sure that, work permitting, I would show up.

So being trapped in the studio on any Thursday afternoon was a real loss, but, though I'd miss Madame for sure, there was still a chance that I'd be finished in time to meet my pal Pyotr. He was foreign, like me, his people Russians who fled after the revolution. They lodged in what he said was appalling squalor out near the Vaugirard slaughterhouses, and Pyotr, who preferred the streets, had become a real Parisian *garçon* despite his broad shoulders and his wide, Slavic face. He was stylish in his own way, a demi-apache look with his neck scarf and striped shirt. He wore a big dark hat and a surly expression, projecting a mostly bogus air of menace that was attractive to the punters.

I saw the charm, although he was too young for my taste, and I was too poor for his. He had no interest in art, either, associating painters with the poverty that he was determined to escape. "Give me a fat wallet any day," he said often enough to make me suspect that he was also a pickpocket. I know that he kept an eye out for the *flics* when we were together, which was reassuring in a way.

What had we in common? Only food. He knew every good, cheap restaurant on the Left Bank, and if we met up, I planned to treat him to a decent dinner since Mother had sent my allowance. This was to be followed by an evening trolling the cafés of Montparnasse, where he would look for trade, and I would try to interest an English-speaking foreigner. Schoolboy exercises of *la plume de ma tante* and *le table de mon oncle* did not prepare me to chat up a French painter—or pick up a French sailor. More's the pity.

But I was learning! Also the decorator's trade, a craft requiring concentration and a steady hand, which that particular day I lacked—a big blotch of indigo paint landed squarely on a beige-and-cream highlight. I exhausted my vocabulary in three languages as I struggled to blot up the paint, then wasted time trying to cover over the remains of the error, a difficult matter in gouache, even if it is opaque. Half an hour later, I gave up, got a new sheet and began the whole tedious exercise again. By the time I was finished, the famous lavender dusk of Paris was fading into darkness, the streetlights were coming on, and my pal Pyotr would already have set his course for Le Select, the Dôme, the Café de la Rotonde, or even the Parnasse Bar, tended by the famous Jimmy, one of my countrymen.

Personally, I favored Le Select, even though my French was too poor yet for real conversation, because the Surrealists met there. Pyotr gave me no help with them, and he even refused to introduce me to the one rather shabby Russian painter he recognized. "No, no, Francis," he said. "It is a life of poverty and misery, fit only for Jews and Frenchmen. Flee it as you would the devil." He was so moved that he broke into Russian, which made him different somehow, more mysterious, more threatening. Pyotr had hidden depths, I suspected, and more to him than the average street hustler. I found that interesting, and I was disappointed to miss him.

Still, the night held promise. Fortified by lamb stew with white beans and a *pichet* of red wine, I ventured along Vaugirard to the boulevard du Montparnasse and the ex-pats' playground. So many Americans, so many English, all rejoicing in the cheap franc. Me, too, although the pound does not stretch as far as the almighty dollar that has brought Yank writers and painters by the boatload.

They came for art and stayed to drink on the cheap and swan around with their money. I disliked their showy wealth, even if a couple of the black chorus boys were marvelous looking, as was Vander Clyde, the Texas aerialist who performed as the gorgeous Barbette on the wire. But they were all workingmen like Pyotr, my guide to *Paris de nuit*, whom I spotted at one of the Dôme's outside tables.

He was sitting with a large, rawboned man wearing a bad suit and a cloth cap. The cap hid the man's eyes but not his heavy ill-shaven jaw and thin, wide mouth. He was not your average boulevardier by any means, and he did not look as if he'd be a profitable companion for Pyotr either. I smelled mysterious Russian politics and gave a wave, intending to walk on, but my friend jumped up and called me over.

"*Mon amie*, Francis," he told his companion, adding, "*Il est l'anglais*," although I'd told him often enough that I'm Irish born.

The man glowered at me, and I rather doubt my reception would have been any different if he'd known I'd sprung from Mother Ireland. He did not respond to my greeting but leaned back in his chair and lit a cigarette before saying something in Russian to Pyotr. He didn't seem happy to see me, and I told Pyotr that I would not stay.

"*Non, non*, Francis," Pyotr said. At this, the mystery man signaled the waiter and ordered me a *vin blanc*.

Had I read the signals wrong? I'd gotten good at scenting hostility in Berlin, but maybe Russian manners were different, because he leaned forward and, in heavily accented French, introduced himself. He was Igor, no surname mentioned, and my friend Pyotr was taking him around to see the sights.

Right. I mentioned the Louvre and Notre-Dame and Luxembourg Garden and Palace, and he nodded as if taking this all in for his next walking tour. Now and again, he spoke to Pyotr in Russian, and I sensed that I was being evaluated in some way.

"*Francis est tres gentil,*" Pyotr said, but I didn't think Igor was too concerned with my manners.

He said something else in Russian, but though Pyotr shook his head, the Russian persisted. After a moment, he turned to me. "We are meeting a friend," he said in slow, rough French. "Three is an irregular number."

I agreed that three could be awkward and tried to exchange glances with Pyotr.

"It would be pleasing if you would join us."

"For a little time, perhaps."

"A walk," said Igor. "*Une promenade.*"

Pyotr said something in Russian but was cut off with a gesture. Igor then ordered another round of *vin blanc*. Pyotr and I sat there looking awkward; Igor, in contrast, now seemed quite at his ease. Our wine disappeared, and I was about to remark on the time, invent another appointment, remember something left undone at Armand's studio, when Igor leaped to his feet and waved over another Russian, this one tall and lean with hollow cheeks and glittering gray eyes behind little gold-rimmed spectacles.

If Igor looked like a street tough or a rustic from some remote farm, Lev suggested a professor or a bureaucrat in exile. His clothes were old, many seasons out of style, but of good quality, and his rapid French sounded polished. When he shook hands, I noticed that his fingers were stained to the second joint: a chain-smoker or a chemist.

I was introduced as an art student. Pyotr got a somewhat longer introduction in Russian, the politics of exiles being as complex as the rules of cricket. The man sat down. He had interesting eyes, and I had time to study them because I seemed of considerable interest to him. *Oh, ho, Francis!* Now I detected a second scenario. While initially I'd figured that Pyotr had wanted me to distract the thuggish Igor, now Igor seemed eager for me to amuse his cultivated friend, making Pyotr either nervous or jealous.

I leaned toward the former, for Lev's hooded eyes gave him a thoughtful, almost sinister, air. He drank a *vin rouge*, and then Igor clapped his hands together with a great show of enthusiasm and suggested a walk. "In the so beautiful Parisian moonlight."

Lev shrugged. There was a moment's silence. Igor looked around the table. I saw Pyotr give the slightest shake of his head. Igor leaned over and put a hand on his neck in a way that was at once proprietary and threatening. Lev's faintly slanted eyes slid toward me, and, in a moment of mischief, I gave him a wink. Not smart but he was a quite fascinating man.

"*Bon,*" said Igor and stood up. He took Pyotr's arm; Lev took mine and we set out. I was not at all surprised when Igor set our course toward the big cemetery with its quiet, dark tree-lined streets. I expected a fumble in the bushes, something quick and exciting between the tombs with profit down the road for at least three of us. That's how I read the tea leaves, but I was quite wrong.

Oh, Lev was interested all right, and I was beginning to find the situation attractive, when Igor stopped. He and Pyotr had been walking a little ahead. I saw him turn as if to call back to us, and in that instant Pyotr plunged into the cemetery, yelling, "*Allez,* Francis."

I was too surprised to react instantly, and when I tried to follow, Lev seized my arm. He said something in Russian and tried to pull me in front of his body. I kicked back and broke free, falling onto my knees on the pavement as there was a bang and a whistle and another bang, deafeningly loud and very close. A scream cut through the reverberation, and I was aware of Lev falling backward.

Those were shots; that whistle, a bullet. Panicked, I scrambled away, crawling until I got to my feet at the curbing, then stumbled toward the shrubs and trees that surrounded the monuments and mausoleums. I lunged for the shadows, tripping over edging around the graves and roots of ancient shrubs, knocking over canisters of flowers and brittle memorial wreaths.

I ran until I could catch my breath. "Pyotr!" More a wheeze than a yell and no answer forthcoming. The moonlight was bright, the shadows inky; the street was out of sight. Gasping amid the grotesque shadows of the tombs, I wanted nothing more than streetlights and pavement and an inside seat at a café, things not to be risked until I was sure that Igor and the gunman were gone. At the memory of the whistling bullets, my heart jumped. How close I'd been to my final resting place.

Think, Francis! That was always Nan's advice in a crisis. Along with *Don't panic*, another helpful thought. I struggled to get my breathing back to normal then moved slowly and carefully among the monuments. My chances of outrunning anyone really fit were slim, and I hoped that whoever had fired the shots would be focused on his own escape. I reached one of the footpaths through the cemetery and, risking the moonlight, headed to where I hoped I would meet the boulevard.

Sounds of running feet sent me back among the tombs, and I crouched in the shadows of what proved to be a large sculptured bed, a monument, apparently to a happy marriage, for it was topped with two figures looking incongruously plump and cheerful. Someone passed down the walk, but I was not able to recognize the figure, and I didn't dare call again to Pyotr. I waited a moment, stood up, and started along the grass. In the distance, I heard a police Klaxon. Coming this way?

Hearing the rising pitch and volume, I charged back into the shadows, only to stumble when a hand reached out of the darkness to grab my leg. I gave a shout and struggled frantically to keep my balance as old Irish ghosts swarmed up from a dozen nursery tales.

"Francis! C'est Pyotr!"

I collapsed wheezing onto the grass, and he asked if I was

hurt. I shook my head, but it was several minutes before I could speak and several more before I could follow his lead on a circuitous route that took us safely out of the cemetery. By this time, we had heard several more police cars arriving, and when we reached the first streetlight, I saw how anxious Pyotr looked.

I stopped and asked, "What was that all about?"

He gave one of the Parisians' all-purpose shrugs. "Politics. I truly did not know there would be shooting."

I didn't ask him exactly what he had expected. "Who were those people?"

He shrugged again. "Igor is a Bolshevik, and Lev is an old Menshevik. One betrayed the other somehow back in Moscow. Politics or money or murder. I thought if you were there that Igor would postpone his plans."

For the moment, I thought it best to believe that, for after all Pyotr had given me warning.

"Have you a room?" he asked after we had gone a couple more blocks.

And when I said I did, he took my arm. "I can't go home now," he said.

CHAPTER TWO

My room was on the fourth floor of a tattered building off Vaugirard. It was cheap and, except for the dirty lavatory and the nosy concierge, a bargain: A double bed, a table, a chair. A sink and bidet, even a window. There was a hook for my coat and my second jacket and a small bureau for my two clean shirts and my underwear. Though hardly the Hotel Adlon, the room had everything I needed for a few francs a day. With my five-pound sterling allowance, I could afford it quite nicely.

"Ah," said Pyotr when we came in. "All the comforts."

Was there an edge to his voice? Should I take warning? Too late now.

I went to the bureau for the bottle of cognac I kept for emergencies. Tonight surely qualified. I poured us each a drink. Pyotr knocked his back and helped himself to another, then sat down on the bed. "You are a true friend, Francis," he said, looking so gloomy that I feared he might burst into tears. Russians are not of the stiff-upper-lip school.

"If you had not shouted," I said.

He nodded. "You'd be dead. Shot." He sighed and rubbed his face. "You must avoid Igor at all costs, Francis."

"And you?"

"I must disappear for a while." He made a face. "Who knows? Maybe the police have caught Igor. Maybe both were shot."

"Maybe Lev survived?"

"That would be worse," Pyotr said. "That would be very bad, indeed." He held out his hand for the cognac and took another swig before kicking off his boots. He lay back on the bed and went to sleep almost instantly. I switched off the light and stood at the window, watching the moonlit street for Russian assassins and *les flics*. A few men wandered by, drunk from the sound of them; a couple of women clattered past in their high heels, a weary and discouraged sound. Otherwise, all quiet. It appeared that no one had followed us out of the tombs and bushes and that my room was as safe as anywhere. For the moment.

I glanced over at Pyotr, who was snoring gently. He felt safe enough and he ought to know. But as I took off my shoes and trousers and slid carefully into bed, I thought I would be happier when he found another bolt-hole.

The night was distinguished by dreams of moonlit sculptures, phantom police Klaxons, and sinister running men. My window had no curtain and, as usual, I woke up as soon as the sun came in. Not so Pyotr. Clearly, he could sleep anywhere and caught his forty winks whenever he could. I pulled on my trousers to visit the lavatory, an appalling "squatter" with an open drain. Why the cultural capital of Europe borrowed these from the Turks is an enduring mystery. They say language is the way to understand a culture, but you can learn a fair bit from the plumbing, too.

Back in my room, I washed my hands and face, put on my jacket, and went downstairs, leaving Pyotr asleep. The old concierge was already up. "*Bonjour, Madame,*" I said, and before she could remark on my visitor, I added that my brother would be leaving in an hour or so.

"*Bon, Monsieur,*" she said, though her look was appropriately skeptical.

At the corner café, I ordered a roll and an espresso at the counter and checked the café's copy of *Le Figaro*: nothing about a shooting in the Cimetière de Montparnasse. Perhaps the incident had been less lethal than Pyotr feared, a dustup not a tragedy. Perhaps Lev had been only slightly wounded. Perhaps he and Igor and anyone else involved had hightailed it before *les flics* arrived.

These were happy thoughts, and the day was looking up until I opened my wallet to pay the barman. My francs were all in order. But what about the second compartment where the bulk of my monthly allowance had rested only the evening before? Empty. I felt my stomach drop. A few pounds sterling meant the difference between relative comfort and poverty—even destitution.

When and where had they vanished? I guessed that sometime in the night those pound notes had migrated from my wallet to Pyotr's pocket. I ran from the café to the flat. The door stood ajar, and Pyotr was gone along with my best jacket and one of my good shirts. I stuck my head out the window, but the street was empty. He must have headed out soon after I left.

I checked the inventory. He'd spared my decent shoes and all my underwear. Also the drawing equipment. Nice of him but not good enough. I was almost shaking with anger to think that if he had just returned my wave, I'd have had an evening on the town and his political troubles would be none of my concern.

But as Nan says, *No use crying over spilled milk.* After a few minutes of fuming, I remembered that his parents supposedly lived out toward the Vaugirard slaughterhouses. I'd probably find him in that dismal and impoverished district, and if I couldn't run him to ground there, surely I'd catch up with him at Le Select or the Dôme. I envisioned an angry scene and didn't rule out a punch-up until I spotted the note.

Je suis désolé, it began. French does make "I'm sorry" sound more intense if not more sincere. He wrote that he was running for his life and in such dire straits he hoped that stealing from a friend might be excused. I doubted his premise although I could see the conclusion followed. *Soyez prudent!* He'd underlined that three times—be careful—and he added as postscript that neither of us had been meant to survive.

I doubted that bit of melodrama. Anyone who picks your pocket is automatically suspect, and Pyotr always came with a certain emotional excess. Playacting, I'd often thought, to go with his gangster air and apache wardrobe. But despite the clear and cheerful morning light, I couldn't quite dismiss the idea, either.

Those had been real shots last night; Lev's cry of pain, genuine; and I had felt real menace from both Igor and Lev even before the attack at the cemetery. Yes, indeed, and the reason for my presence. Without a sinister edge, Igor would have been merely one of the great unwashed, and Lev, a seedy chap down on his luck. *Be careful*, I told myself, *is good advice.*

I read the message again, this time noticing Pyotr's beautiful handwriting and correct grammar. Somewhere along the line, he'd had more education than he pretended, and that made me wonder what else he'd concealed. Maybe he'd lied about his ignorance of Russian politics and about Lev and Igor. Possibly they weren't even Reds at all but members of some White Russian faction well known to him. There were many such exiles in Paris, and I'd assumed from the first that Pyotr's people were old czarists or some non-Bolshevik revolutionaries.

A political morass for certain, but I was loath to lose the allowance that kept me independent. My first thought was to search for Pyotr immediately, and my second was to hope for his return. I was still dithering when the church bell rang for eight thirty, and I had to postpone my decision: Armand expected the apprentice to be in on the dot.

When I arrived at the studio, *le maître* was all business, dressed up very swank with a high collar and spotless cuffs and a good deal of jewelry. His hair had been quite transformed by pomade, and his cane with its polished silver head was at the ready: He had a lunch meeting with an important client. With the exception of the finishing touches on my irises, all was in readiness. He sat me down to add highlights on the final variation, golds, yellows, creams, and chartreuse with a few strengthening touches of sienna, while he packed the rest of the proposed designs in two big portfolios.

I half hoped I'd be taken along to carry these; I could enjoy a fine meal at a fancy restaurant. Armand dismissed my hints with a wave. He had, *naturellement*, hired a cab to take the work. "But you may have the rest of the day off," he said. Then he had me check the back of his jacket and trousers and make sure that all was flawless. "*Bonne*," I said. "*Et bonne chance.*"

He sniffed. "Armand does not need luck, just intelligent clients." With this, he signaled for me to bring the work and swept downstairs to the waiting cab. I loaded the portfolios, Armand got in beside them, and there I was, free for the day just before noon. Clearly, I was fated to begin my search for Pyotr and my missing pounds.

But first, a stop at a café for a little pick-me-up—another of Armand's insinuating expressions—and more important, for a look at the later editions of the papers. Reports of a ghastly murder in the *cimetière* and my expedition would be called off. If not, *Onward, Francis.* I checked not one but two papers and hastily skimmed a third—was I taking Pyotr's warnings too much to heart? I reminded myself that the smartest thing he could have done was to put the wind up me and so avoid pursuit. With this in mind, I set out.

The area hit my nose on the outskirts: a nasty, primal smell. Not the smell familiar to country people of the long dead fox, rabbit, or dog carcass discovered by the roadside, but the mingled odors of terrified sudden death. I suspected that the morning slaughter was finished, for there were no animals being driven through the streets, no cattle trucks moving, no screams of fear or pain. Just the odor. I could see why Pyotr preferred a precarious life on the streets of Montparnasse.

I carried a sketchpad and a box of pencils that I'd borrowed from Armand's. This was one of the many things the apprentice was forbidden to do, but a painter's smock and sketchbook served as carte blanche in much of the city. I'd already decided that my boss had employed Pyotr as a model and that I'd been sent to fetch him. I thought that *mon français* was up to the task, and, at every *tabac* and café I passed, I inquired for Pyotr Golubov.

The name didn't produce the slightest recognition until I arrived at a shabby little *tabac* within sound of the rumble and whistle of the railroads. The owner was dark and stooped. He shook his head, which had hairline well past the tide mark, then asked *"Russe?"*

When I nodded, he pointed down the street. *"Le café Trois Étoiles. Plusieurs de Russe."*

I thanked him and walked on. Aside from the distant sound of trains, the district was quiet and the streets empty except for a few women carrying groceries or laundry; some horse carts with vegetables, scrap, or old furniture; and a workman with a ladder, accompanied by a boy with a big can of paste and a roll of paper. No doubt the apprentice for a bill poster. I gave him a nod.

A few minutes later, I spotted Trois Étoiles, a one-story stone building with shutters reaching the sidewalk and something askew about the door and window frames. A couple of chairs and tables sat on the dusty strip adjoining the sidewalk, and several aggressive trees crowded the facade and sprawled across the roof.

The interior was low and so dim after the bright afternoon

light that I did not at first notice that several tables were occupied. I ordered a roll and a *vin blanc* from the barman, tall with jet hair, sharp features, and a quizzical expression. Would he know a Pyotr Golubov?

I got a blank look in return.

I said that Golubov had been hired as a model but had missed a session.

This produced a shrug.

I said I believed he lived in the area.

"Yes, lots of Russians," said the barman, whose French was strongly accented. He looked over the room and said something to the customers in Russian then shook his head. "No one knows a Pyotr Golubov," he said. He turned away to wipe the bar and got so busy among his bottles and glasses that I was sure he was lying.

I left the café with nothing but suspicions and a hole in my wallet. Still, I was clearly in the right area, and the worn buildings, dusty café, and gnarled trees could be considered picturesque. I decided to linger in the little square that overlooked the front door of the Trois Étoiles. While urban vignettes were hardly my interest, it presented just the sort of local color that attracted commercially minded painters. I sat down on a bench and opened up the sketchpad.

A few lines for the buildings. A smudge of shading for the trees. Armand would turn this into a toile pattern and add some lively figures. Perhaps a girl with an old-fashioned laundry basket or a sprightlier version of the sad horses and carts. I find all that boring. I have trouble with perspective, and despite some sessions at figure drawing, I find human anatomy a great challenge—but interesting. Bodies and emotions, that's the thing, both on canvas and in life. Particularly strong emotions.

Maybe that was why I had gone for that ill-advised walk with the Russians. Maybe that was why I was watching the door of the café. Within minutes, three heavy-shouldered men came out. They stood talking amid the tables until a fourth emerged. He wore a cloth cap like Igor, and I had a moment's alarm before I realized that this man looked smaller and thinner. He said something to the others and walked off toward the rail lines. His companions remained talking, a discussion that involved big gestures and raised voices. I was relieved that they were so engrossed that they did not notice me before they left down the narrow street that ran beside the café.

I followed them into a warren of small, dark streets with companionable buildings leaning against each other for support. The road was dirty, the facades dark with smoke, and all was permeated by the distinctive stink of French drains. Shortly, I reached a more open area, perhaps a park in better times, for there were tree stumps scattered between the ramshackle buildings.

The men from the café were clearly residents. They hollered greetings in Russian as they passed each building and waved to the shirtless men playing football or sprawled in the sun with bottles of wine or vodka. The regularly spaced buildings had some surprising decorative elements, suggesting the pavilions of an old amusement area long fallen into neglect. The sagging roofs were missing tiles, and nearly every building had at least one broken window, usually with an exhaust pipe puffing coal smoke to darken the grayish sheets and yellow underwear drying on lines between the buildings.

Glass crunched underfoot, but that did not deter the bare-foot children, scantily clad and dirty legged, who raced about followed by skinny dogs. Women in thin slippers or wooden clogs went in and out with baguettes under their arms and baskets with cabbages and onions. I'd feared I might stand out, but I saw several men wearing paint-stained smocks. Surely I was near the artists' colony Pyotr had mentioned. If so, I was dressed just right.

A high wall set off what might once have been a garden, and I soon reached an elegant iron gate set amid the ivy. Visible through the bars was a remarkable three-story octagonal building with a complicated roof, decorative sculptures, and a balustrade. Although in disrepair, the building and what had once been its grounds seemed incongruous amid the slatternly compound. Could this be *La Ruche*, the famous "Beehive" of the older avant-garde?

In my excitement, I forgot the Russians. I skirted piles of litter, including fragments of a stone carving—this was definitely the place!—and squeezed past shacks, even flimsier than the rest, that leaned against the wall. Beyond one of them, a small iron door had been propped ajar. I had just stepped onto the paved forecourt when the door banged shut behind me. I glanced back to see two men with wide shoulders and broad Slavic faces, patrons of that charming café, Trois Étoiles.

Toughs for sure and normally just my type, but today I wasn't susceptible to their charm. "You," one said in French. "What you want with Pyotr?"

"He owes us a modeling session," I said, shifting my arm so that he could see my sketchpad.

The man gave a coarse laugh. "Modeling, my ass. Or rather his."
He laughed again and so did his friend.

"You're maybe his friend, yes? You maybe know where that little"—and here he broke into Russian but I still got the point—"is hiding. Yes?"

"No," I said. "I'm looking for him myself."

"But you come here," he said.

"I followed you. You're Russian, I thought you might know. But if not—" I moved a step farther. "I won't take your time."

This produced another laugh. "We have all the time in the world. But you, *tovarisch*, you don't have time. Not if you are a friend of Pyotr's."

With this he grabbed my arm and twisted it behind my back. I stamped on his foot—I've found I quite like rough men, but I've no time for bullies. He gave a yell and a hop. I dropped my sketchpad and twisted away but not before a fist landed against my ribs, and I caught a glimpse of a close-cropped hair, blond stubble, a scarred temple.

This one was demanding answers in Russian. Good luck with that. The only words I understood were Pyotr and Igor, but I knew I was in big trouble. I swung my free arm wildly and connected at least once, producing another flurry of blows.

The other man was screaming at me in French: "*Où est Pyotr?*"

"I don't know! He stole four pounds from me!" I cried in English, danger causing my *français* to take French leave along with my common sense. I felt blood in my mouth, and I had fallen to my knees when the main door of the Beehive creaked opened.

A shouted warning with an added bouquet of pungent French.

The blows stopped. I got my hands on the pavement, levered myself upright, and scrambled for the open doorway. Two men stood there. One carried a mason's mallet and looked to have the muscles to use it. The other was a rawboned chap hauling a big chunk of stone on a wooden dolly.

"*Au secours!*" I shouted, and the man with the mallet stepped aside. In my haste, I knocked my shin on the dolly and tumbled inside a big, round space, lit by a dirty skylight high overhead. The two Russians thought to follow but if the shouts in Russian, French, and Italian were any indication, the sculptors were no friends of theirs. Good. But better would be an exit. There were doors evenly spaced all the way around the room, and I tried one after another without success. Outside, the Russian voices grew more insistent, and I was considering the rickety stairs to the second level when a door swung open.

A thin face with a long beak of a nose, black hair, bony cheeks, a stubble of beard, and remarkable black, fathomless eyes. Then a hand, thinner than the face with long fingers, paint stained at the tips, beckoned. "*Vite! Vite! Les Cosaques!*" I didn't hesitate to jump inside. He ran a sturdy board between two heavy staples, then motioned for me to sit on the sole chair, a wooden contraption with uneven legs and a cracked back.

I sat down to assess the damage. There was blood on my face. A tooth was looser than it had been at lunchtime, and my left side burned. They say broken ribs heal stronger. I hoped so. My breath sounded like a broken-winded horse, and the peculiar stench in the room did nothing to help my struggling lungs.

When he saw my distress, the painter rummaged among his tubes, brushes, and cans for an inky-looking bottle of wine. He poured some into a glass and held it out. "*Boire*," he said.

I did and coughed. It was a remote relative of rotgut, but it shocked my lungs back to cooperation. "*Merci.*"

He grunted and, after a quick glance out the window, returned to work at his large easel, seemingly quite incurious about either my arrival or my appearance. After a few minutes, I recovered enough to stand up and look around. The studio was spacious and well lit, but the broken panes in the big windows must let in a frightful amount of cold. The improvised shutters protecting the lower part of the windows and the extra barrier on the door suggested undesirable neighbors, perhaps *les Cosaques*. The floor was filthy with paint stains and littered with old sketches and empty bottles. But that did not account for the truly sinister odor that permeated the room.

I took a step forward and saw the canvas. Although only medium size, it was the most brutal and vigorous thing I'd seen in France: a dead rooster splayed on a greenish-black ground. The clawed feet were almost of human expressiveness as was the massive beak, open in an almost human scream. Then I noticed the model: the carcass of a fowl many days dead.

"*C'est formidable*," I said, although I had not intended to disturb him.

"You like?"

"Very much." When I added that I had seen nothing so vivid since Berlin, he wiped his brush and put it in a jar of turps. He picked up his painting stool and motioned for me to return to his sitting area. He poured us each another glass.

"I'm not able to travel to see as much as I'd like at the moment. But if you'd be so kind as to describe the work in Berlin—"

I said I'd like nothing better, except to see some more of his work.

"In time," he said.

With this promise, I launched into an account of everything good I'd seen in Berlin. He had me repeat the painters' names and asked for detailed descriptions of the works that interested him. I really had to concentrate to convey the density of the canvases and the eccentric drawing in my limited French. At one point, I had to pick up a pencil to give him some idea of the open line and ferocious caricatures of George Grosz.

"They are painting the war," he said when my report had satisfied him.

"The war, the aftermath. Many disasters."

"And what's to come? Are they painting what's yet to come, eh?"

I shrugged. I was barely eighteen—what did I know.

"It's what's to come," he said and actually wrung his hands. Then he took another slug of the wine—his digestion must be cast iron—and walked over to the side wall where dozens of canvases were stacked. He turned a couple face out for me.

These were finished works, heavy with impasto, the paint laid on with thick ropy strokes, all conveying the most violent emotion. I was impressed and said so. He nodded without speaking. I wondered what it would be like to be that good—and possibly to know you were good—and to be living in squalor with marvelous work that had no market.

Armand's dictum, *The market is God*, was in my ear when the painter turned over a portrait: a boy roughly my age in a striped shirt with a raw, shifty expression—definitely a shifty expression. He was leaning back on a chair with his legs apart, and the wild brushstrokes brought him vividly to life. "Pyotr," I said.

"You know him?"

"I've seen him around. He's why I came here. He owes me money."

"Stay away from him. A bad type. One of the Cossacks."

I must have looked dubious.

"You see what they do," he said, nodding toward me.

"But surely not all Russians." Even if it was at the last minute, Pyotr had given me warning at some risk to himself.

"They are all Cossacks if you're a Jew," he said. Something in his tone told me I'd overstayed my welcome, and I said that I should go.

Without any response, he opened the door. Before I could properly say good-bye, he had closed it behind me and clattered down the bar, leaving me in the gloomy atrium. Murky light filtering through decades of dust. A faint whiff, still, of the painter's dead subject, mingling with the odor of paint and thinner. The sound, close by, of metal hitting stone. I looked out the cracked and patched the front door. No sign of the "Cossacks." Were they waiting beyond the wall? I was trying to decide the best line of retreat, when someone called, "*Monsieur.*"

It was my savior, the mason. I turned back to thank him for my timely rescue.

"It was nothing," he said in polite French, and looking at his massive physique and the ease with which he held the heavy mallet,

I could believe that seeing off a couple of toughs was easy for him.

"Your face," he said and motioned me inside. His studio had a washbasin, and he let me clean up. "That is better," he said when I had dried my hands and face on a scrap of towel. "You look fit to meet the world."

"Your neighbor treated only the inner man."

"I thought I smelled some of his wine. Lucky you are still on your feet. I think he makes it himself. Poor Chaim is a genius but very eccentric."

He shook his head and handed me my sketchpad and the bundle of pencils.

"Thanks. They are mostly just wallpaper variations, but my boss would have been furious."

"One must live." Then, as if he sensed my apprehension, he added, "I have only a little more to do this afternoon before I'm off. Wait, if you don't mind the noise and dust. No one will bother you if you walk with me."

CHAPTER THREE

I had a drink with the mason, whom I should properly call a sculptor, as he has serious ambitions and interesting ideas. This was at his local café, where I bought us *sandwich jambons* in an effort to sop up the nearly toxic wine I'd drunk. The sculptor leaned against the bar, and said, "Simplify, simplify," as his large hands shaped the air into graceful curves. He was a poet and intellectual who aspired to pure shapes and *le aerodynamic* forms. Women, men, birds were to be reduced to their essences and captured in stone.

A fascinating idea and potentially beautiful, too, if the half-completed work on his stand was any indication. But not for me. I don't think the pure and the beautiful will ever be my terrain. There are too many flaws and too much dirt and mess in life for that. Still, that afternoon counted as a red-letter day in my art education, and on the way back to my room, I bought Nan a postcard showing the banks of the Seine with Notre-Dame rising in the background.

I send Nan a postcard every time I see something really interesting, and while the view of the Seine is a good deal more decorative than the artists' colony, I knew that she would enjoy it more. *All well. Met interesting painter and a sculptor today! Mon français is improving. Love, Francis.*

I could, of course, have told her of my latest adventures. I can tell Nan anything, but gunshots and thugs and what appeared to be a loose tooth would only worry her and make things seem worse just when, thanks to my visit to the sculptor's café, the events of the afternoon no longer looked so serious. Even the night in the cemetery might have receded into memory if I hadn't passed a news kiosk splashed with headlines all telling the same tale: SHOOTING VICTIM DISCOVERED IN CIMITIÈRE DE MONTPARNASSE.

With a psychic jolt, the good effects of the grape vanished. I'd been kidding myself. One of the Russians had been killed, murdered, deliberately assassinated. Pyotr was in danger, and I was both in danger and broke. That counted as trouble on a number of fronts. My favorite boulevard cafés were out. If Igor was looking for me, those would be the natural place for him to begin. No cafés meant no chance of a free-spending boulevardier or sensation-seeking tourist. I'd better hope I could coax an advance out of Armand.

In the meantime, head down, Francis. I returned to my room in daylight—a miserable novelty—and showed up bright and early at Armand's. I worked late, too, because his lunch meeting had been a great success and I had more tulip variations to paint. By the end of the day, I had hostile feelings toward Dutch bulb growers and most of the Netherlands.

A visit to Shakespeare and Company to borrow a book. Fortunately, they already knew me there and I was trusted. A small dinner at a small restaurant, courtesy of Armand who was moved by my battered face and a tale (false in detail if true in substance) of being assaulted by thugs just after I'd collected my allowance. He didn't necessarily believe my account, but he parted with a few francs and a great deal of advice. Then home to bed.

After a few days of this regimen, I was ready to risk anything for the pleasure of going out on the town. What's the point of living like a monk in a cell—and in Paris, no less! I was sick of my room, and when I left Armand's on Tuesday, I'd convinced myself that all was well, that the Russians, Cossacks or not, had gone to ground, and I could come out of hiding.

"Monsieur Bacon." The dulcet tones of my concierge, a nosy biddy of the first water.

"Madame." I waved and started up the stair.

"You have company," she said. She disapproved of visitors in principle.

I stopped. I was expecting no one.

"Foreign," she said.

"English? American?"

She gave a sly smile. "Russian. Two."

One was bad, two was twice as bad. "Upstairs?"

She shrugged. "They were most persuasive, Monsieur."

"Tell them I've never come back," I said and parted with a franc.

"That is understood, Monsieur."

"And when they leave, if you would pack and bring down my things."

She looked indignant. She was not a chambermaid.

"Then you can rent the room. Immediately. I will come by and collect my bag tomorrow."

"*D'accord, Monsieur*," she said with a nod.

I was prepared for an uncomfortable night at the train station, and the whole business would have been a total loss if not for a handsome conductor. He looked sharp in his SNCF uniform and he had beautiful strong legs and a key to a disused carriage. I will forever think kindly of the French rail system.

I left with the dawn, collected my bag, and showed up at Armand's with all my worldly goods and the excuse of working late to finish up the fabric designs. I'd expected him to be delighted, but although the afternoon was interrupted by carrying on around the modeling stand, I could tell that he'd rather have me gone. Perhaps he had someone else in mind for the ivy wreath and the Bacchic dancer.

No matter. I was weary of the textile designs, which seemed thin stuff after the paintings I'd seen.

I hurried my work on Thursday, and when Armand left earlier than expected, I followed as soon as he was out of sight, eager to tell Madame Dumoulin about my discoveries.

"Francis! You've met with an accident!" Madame said when she saw me outside the Louvre. My tooth had settled in again, but I still had bruises on my face and a healing lip.

"A sort of accident. I had some money stolen from me and when I went to get it back—voilà."

She was properly alarmed and sympathetic.

"But, Madame Dumoulin, it was all worthwhile because I made some wonderful discoveries." I pushed *mon français* to the utmost to describe the remarkable work I'd seen, so that I wound up in front of the *Nike of Samothrace* waving my hands to describe the fat lines of paint that re-created the dead rooster and the big pulse of vitality that ran through the painter's work. "Words cannot describe," I finally admitted.

"Words *can* describe," she said, "but not your French. I have thought for a while, Francis, that your work with Monsieur Armand, while very valuable for your technique, is not the best thing for your language."

"Monsieur Armand is usually a man of few words," I admitted. *Except*, I thought, *during his "photo" sessions, but the vocabulary I picked up then was not so generally useful.*

"You rent a room?"

I nodded.

"You should be living with a French family where you will hear correct French morning and night. Now, what I propose, is that you come and live with us for a month, a month at least."

"Oh, Madame! I couldn't impose!" I said, but I knew that I jolly well could. This was wonderful.

"Nonsense," she said. "I know that you would make yourself useful. My son is learning English. You could help him and he could help you. And my brother, Jules"—she hesitated a moment—"he always needs a hand with some project or other. Does that sound too difficult?"

"It sounds charming," I said. "I am truly grateful."

The next morning, as soon as I finished some textile designs for Armand, I took the train toward Fontainebleau and the small town where Madame Dumoulin had a fine stone house, stout and square, painted the palest yellow with gray-green shutters and a red tile roof. I was to have a room of my own, and both the food and the company were excellent. I sat down promptly at my table to send Nan my address.

My dear Nan,

I have fallen into a great piece of luck. My gallery-going friend has invited me to stay. Madame Dumoulin is a widow whose husband was killed in the very last month of the war. He left her several rental properties as well as the family home and everything about the household is agreeable. Besides Madame, there is her son, Luc, thirteen. If you can, please send me on any one of the Herbert Strang annuals as that would be a good English text for him.

There is also Jules, Madame's brother. He is much younger than Madame and was "unsettled" as she puts it by the war.

I paused for a moment, uncertain what to say about Jules, who I liked but who was certainly peculiar enough to defeat any easy assessment. He was big and handsome like Madame but troubled by a cough and spells of weakness that made me think he had been gassed. Despite these problems, he was restlessly active both mentally and physically. He rose early every morning. If there were repairs to be made at any of the rented properties, he set out with his tool kit, and if it was collection day, he took a purse and returned with the rents. Otherwise, he retired to the old horse barn for his current project, because he needed to be working with his hands nearly every waking minute.

He had started, Madame said, right after he was demobilized with carving spoons—hundreds of them. Then he turned wooden bowls by the dozens, one for every house in the village. For a time he made boats, canoes and dinghies and little sailing craft, one of which still lay under a tarp in a disused stall. After that it was furniture, chiefly chairs that were neatly made and ornamented with curious designs. They populated the bedrooms, including mine.

There had been a kite phase, too, including box kites of amazing size and complexity, as well as fighting kites, designed to be maneuverable enough to cut the strings of opponents' fliers. Some of these were painted with exotic designs in bright colors, others, which I found a bit peculiar, carried the features of favorite singers and actresses copied from press and program photographs pasted in his voluminous scrapbooks.

But recently he had embarked on some more interesting, if more troubling, creations: elaborate machines, beautifully made of wood and metal, that performed meaningless tasks. One, when wound up, hammered pegs into holes. This was in progress when I arrived, and Jules was putting the finishing touches on the pegs, shaping them into little figures of soldiers. I was enlisted to paint their uniforms.

There was another machine that dug up earth at the front and filled it in back at the rear. It moved in a circular track and turned up bits of bone and metal. And there was a miniature artillery piece that shot pellets across the room before collapsing to open like a flower. At the press of the button, it closed up again and was ready to reload. These sinister toys were occupying him more and more, Madame said, and who knew what that meant. You can see why I found it hard to give Nan a complete account of Jules Dumoulin.

Sometimes, Jules needed an assistant, and I qualified, having worked with Armand, although there were never going to be any frolics in the workshop with Jules. At least I don't think so. He seemed very taken with certain female entertainers, although occasionally when we were alone, he acted as if we shared some big secret. What might that be but for certain preferences? Maybe so, but, fortunately, he was not my type. The Dumoulin household was as close to living in a happy family as I was ever going to get, and I intended to be the perfect guest, unexceptionable and agreeable in every way.

So I frequently spent my mornings sanding pieces of wood or painting designs or holding various struts and cables, work I found interesting, because Jules talked at length if he had a receptive audience. His eyes alight, his long, clever hands in motion, his handsome face animated, he would explain the construction of a mortise or the proper dimensions of a kite, or some other matter that had caught his attention. I thought that he must have been destined for the classroom before he became "unsettled."

Thanks to his humorous turns of phrase, I began to understand French jokes and metaphors, and I picked up an assortment of odd facts and ideas. Jules had a magpie mind that seized on everything unusual, from stories in the local press to formulas in his late brother-in-law's math or engineering books. Usually, I found no connections among these tidbits, but I suspect he did, for he was very clever and often wore a sly, inward sort of smile as if he understood something no one else did.

That was Jules when he was in the mood, smart and amusing, a born teacher, potentially a success in half a dozen fields. But sometimes the workshop remained shut, and he was a different man altogether, his restless energy switched off like a light. He would sink into the torpor that worried Madame, rousing himself only to play cards: obsessive games of solitaire if he was alone, poker or bridge if there was company.

Madame, solicitous of her brother in most ways, was bored by cards, so on those days, Jules and I played poker for kitchen matches, and I gradually learned to play well enough to be distracting, if not amusing. For this, Madame was grateful. I didn't know how Jules had occupied himself at these times before I arrived, but playing cards for matches was apparently an improvement.

"He was such a sweet boy," she said to me one day. "And then the war."

I had no real idea of the war, just of the aftermath. That was bad enough.

"We cannot judge," she added.

I nodded. Certainly my own life would have been easier with that doctrine.

We play cards, I wrote to Nan, knowing she would enjoy that, being very sharp at bridge, *and he is very much a gentleman.* That would also please her, the one conventional thing about my old nanny being her insistence on courtesy. Very properly, too, as one gets away with a lot if one's manners are impeccable. Leaving

Jules as an "unsettled gentleman," I closed my letter to Nan and began one to my mother. Madame Dumoulin had already written one to her—*No, no, Francis, I must, of course, write to Madame Bacon. She must be assured that you are in a respectable household. She will naturally be concerned.*

As far as concern went, I thought that she should really write to Nan, but I put her note, along with a translation, into the envelope with my latest letter to Mother. I didn't write often—and neither did she—but I wanted an advance on my allowance so I could buy some little gifts for the household. In the meantime, I earned my keep with English lessons, charm, and card games, and I visited the neighborhood cafés only in the company of Jules, whose well-known eccentricities and his supposed eye for the ladies kept me on the straight and narrow.

Such careful living paid off. *Mon français* developed quickly. Soon I was having easy conversations about complicated paintings with Madame and even negotiating a better deal with Armand for the piecework I collected every Thursday when I escorted Madame to Paris. Even Luc's English picked up after Nan sent me two annuals, *The Adventures of Harry Rochester* and *Round the World in Seven Days.*

Madame was checking her mail when I opened the parcel. I'd expected a new book. These were both old and well used.

She saw my face. "What is it, Francis?"

I opened one and showed her the still half-formed handwriting inside: *This book belongs to Francis.*

"Oh, it was yours. Would you rather keep these and not give them to Luc?"

"No, I am delighted. I think he will enjoy them. But Madame, Nan saved these for years. She does not have a big trunk."

Madame understood at once and put her hand on my shoulder. "And my parents let her go," I said and walked out into the garden. Half an hour later, it was Jules who came out, cigarette in hand. "There is a thought," he said, "that time and space are one thing not two." With this preliminary, he proceeded to explain a difficult and obscure theory concerning clocks and the speed of light and the immensity of space, of which only the idea of immensity has stayed with me. "I find the universe comforting," he said. "The bigness of it. My sister finds all that horrible, I mean the infinite distances, the innumerable stars."

He glanced at me and I shrugged.

"To think that we and our sorrows and troubles and sins are as motes in the sun consoles me." He took another drag on his cigarette and watched the smoke spiral above the roses. "Of course, one cannot think of such things too often," he added, and I understood that in his own way he was sympathetic.

"Maybe one should not think too much about anything," I said.

"Maybe one should go for a drink."

I agreed this was a capital idea and we set off for the café where normally Jules flirted with the pretty waitress and exchanged gossip with the locals. Monsieur Jules was popular, and now that my French was better, I could see that his odd habits and obsessive enthusiasms counted among the notable features of the neighborhood, right up beside a few historic houses, fine gardens, and superlative bloodstock. "What are you up to these days, Monsieur Jules," was the usual greeting, and when he was in fine form, Jules was happy to oblige, being a sort of one-man lecture institute.

But that particular night he returned greetings with a friendly wave, took a seat in the shadowed courtyard, and nursed a *vin blanc*. He had learned from Madame Dumoulin of my plan to set up in London with Nan, and after a long silence, he told me I should by all means pursue what he termed my "interesting course." "A man needs to be independent," he said, "and that means money."

I had to agree, though anyone seemingly less concerned with money than Jules would be hard to find.

Perhaps he read my thoughts, for he said, "I've spent too long on my various projects without bringing any of them to profit. Even when I might have. Do not make my mistake."

He looked terribly gloomy, and I ventured to remark that he was still young.

"Indeed," he said. "And I have some thoughts in mind to change my way of life. It is time."

"Timing is all," I agreed. He ordered more wine, and we had a long and deep discussion about timing and time and independence and other topics and agreed so well that I decided that in my next letter to Nan, I would tell her that Jules was a fine chap.

CHAPTER FOUR

For six weeks, everything was lovely in the garden, as Nan would say, and I count my time at Madame Dumoulin's as one of my happiest. But with my French vastly improved and my wallet still light, I decided to return to Paris, confident that Pyotr's sinister friends would have given up and that it would be safe to return to my favorite cafés and usual habits. I told Madame Dumoulin I needed a job and more contacts in the design business. For those, I needed Monsieur Armand.

She kissed me on both cheeks in the French manner and asked me to come once a month for Sunday dinner and to meet her as usual on Thursdays at the galleries. I was delighted to agree. I caught a train to Paris with a light heart, convinced, contrary to all my experience, that I was set for smooth sailing.

And at first, everything went swimmingly. The cafés were still full of the rich and idle, some of whom were happy to make my life agreeable. With my new command of the language, I was able to follow the artistic debates at Le Select and the other cafés favored by painters, even if I was too shy to contribute. Work was fine, too. Armand had suffered a romantic setback during my absence and now recognized my virtues. He raised my pay by a few francs and assigned me the preliminary designs for rugs with the promise of a crack at some furniture designs. Since I'd been coached by Jules on the finer points of chair construction, I anticipated no problems there.

Weeks passed in this pleasant manner. I saw no sign of Pyotr or the sinister Russians. I built up a portfolio and cultivated Philip, a wealthy English antiques dealer, who I hoped might help me to a studio in London. After my hand-to-mouth existence in Berlin, Paris in the spring was everything I could desire. I dispatched postcards by the handful to Nan and began to imagine us both in London before winter.

Naturellement, as Armand would say, such good fortune couldn't last, and I was not totally surprised when it didn't. I shouldn't have been surprised by the agent of misfortune either, but I was, which showed that I don't always have as much foresight as I like to think. In any case, complications did not arrive with a thunderclap. Rather, what became big problems crept in with a stealthy accumulation of small incidents. The first came when I was at a small café with my English antique dealer. Philip was a familiar type: rich and free spending abroad; timid and discreet at home. I saw him as promising and presented myself as a discerning "gentleman's gentleman," adding a few years to my age in hopes of seeming more stable and sophisticated.

Whether that ploy worked or not, I soon found that he was interested in new art, and there, I could oblige. Thanks to Madame Dumoulin, I knew every select gallery, and, thanks to my excursion to the Beehive, I had lines to a number of studios. In return, Philip took me out for fine dinners with expensive wine, so that my palate, neglected since the Hotel Adlon of delightful memory, began to revive. We strolled the boulevards and took in racy vaudeville shows and saw many performances by the remarkable aerialist Barbette. All this was good.

Even better was the fact that the four- and five-star restaurants Philip favored were unlikely to attract undesirables like Igor and the Cossacks from the Beehive. I felt safe with Philip, and I began to let down my guard. Mistake! One evening, we were having an aperitif at a modest café, preparatory for what Philip liked to call "a night on the town," when I looked over and saw, to my alarm—better make that to my horror—a shock of dyed red hair, a tatty beret, an ill-cut French suit: my uncle Lastings.

I'd last seen him on a train out of the Weimar Republic, when the old hypocrite had the nerve to congratulate me for traveling at official expense—as if deportation were a species of Cook's tour. He'd already become French by then, which was no doubt the safest way for him to leave Berlin, and he'd hinted at plans, no doubt as fraudulent as his last scheme, that had very nearly gotten us murdered.

Had he seen me? I feared he had. *Know your terrain* was one of his catchphrases, and I have to say that, like a good soldier, the old bastard rarely let himself be taken by surprise. But he was French now and might not want to recognize his Anglo-Irish nephew. That was my hope, along with getting off to dinner as fast as possible. I glanced at Philip in a meaningful way and made to rise, but he'd begun a conversation with the adjoining table.

Philip's French was excellent (another attraction in my view) and he had a friendly, open manner that I guessed made him successful in a trade that relies as much on plausibility as provenance.

The few remarks they exchanged were just time enough for Uncle Lastings to put some coins on the saucer, push back his chair, and approach our table. I was prepared to deny our acquaintance when, to my surprise, he greeted Philip enthusiastically.

"*Ah, bon soir*, Claude," Philip replied, rising to shake my uncle's hand.

Claude! My foot.

"And this is Francis, who has been showing me the little galleries known only to Parisians and clever art students."

"*Bon soir*, Francis," he said and gave my hand a little extra squeeze. He really was incorrigible. I have to admit that my uncle's accent passed muster. For the moment, he was not my lecherous uncle but a Frenchman named Claude who had some business in mind and whose French was almost too rapid for me to follow.

"A boule chest?" I heard Philip say. "Ormolu mounts? Those do very well in London—if pre-1830."

Here, Claude shrugged. "Might be later, but the ormolu is the real thing. Not every workshop obeyed the mercury prohibition, you know."

"Indeed." Philip gave a little laugh. "What would our trade be with strict legality? Genuine ormolu, yes, I might be interested. Francis and I might come and have a little look."

"*D'accord*," said my uncle, and when he thought Philip wasn't looking, he gave me a wink. Uncle Lastings had something up his sleeve all right, and I was unsurprised when I spotted him outside Armand's studio two days later. He was standing under a chestnut tree smoking one of his vile Gauloises.

"Francis!"

"Uncle Lastings. Or am I to call you Claude?"

"Needs must. It's Claude at the moment."

"And what do you want?"

"Now, now, let us not drop family feeling along with the name," my uncle said, and he took my arm. "I want a little advice, as it turns out, and I'll treat you to a slap-up meal in exchange. Though I can see that you're doing all right for yourself. As I knew you would, my boy. Did I not say that you were remarkable?"

I was in no mood for my uncle's cynical flattery. "Why do you wear that horrible suit? And the dyed hair. Red is not a good color for you."

"I see I never discussed deep cover with you, Francis. Of course, your uncle Lastings would never appear in anything but Savile Row and his own hair. But Claude is someone else entirely."

I wasn't so sure of that. I figured that, dye job or not, he was certainly up to something.

Just the same, he got us a good dinner. My uncle shared Pyotr's talent for finding modest restaurants with excellent kitchens. We had salads and rabbit and a good wine plus a handsome gateau, and I was beginning to warm to my uncle when he remarked, "Philip thinks well of you."

"I'd like that to continue," I said.

"Sensible boy. He's quite well off with excellent contacts. Whether or not you have enough discretion for him in London—"

"Is not really your concern."

"My boy! Our good times have clearly slipped your memory! *Où sont les neiges d'antan?*"

My uncle quoting poetry was also new. I hadn't realized that French could affect one in quite that way.

"*Ah, quel dommage!* I see you do not know François Villon, the poet thief of the Middle Ages. A man with an appreciation for the tricks and losses of time. Right up your alley, I should think, Francis."

He gave a wolfish smile. As Lastings, he had been the bluff military man. As Claude, he was sly, inclined to quote poetry, and, given enough time, possibly set to venture into philosophy. But now he took out a little notebook. "Philip mentioned that you had taken him around the galleries."

I nodded, suddenly glad I had not credited my excursions to Madame Dumoulin, because a prosperous widow of handsome appearance would be an irresistible target for him, and a meeting between her and my uncle could only end in embarrassment.

"So," he said, "who are the artists of the moment. Big names."

"Big names? Picasso, Matisse; they don't get any bigger than that. Braque, I like, and Gris, too. Are you thinking of buying? Those are expensive. What about Soutine? Soutine is cheap at the moment but will be valuable in time. I'm sure of it."

"Let's stick with the gilt-edged ones, my boy."

"Dufy is popular. Lightweight but popular. Vuillard is

decorative, so is Bonnard. Bonnard is better, although Vuillard is more peculiar."

He wrote these down.

"Derain, another Fauve—bright unrealistic colors and simplified shapes," I added, when I saw that the term meant nothing. "Marquet, likewise."

I included the names of some able younger painters before my uncle folded up the notebook. "Excellent," he said. "I can honestly say I have never regretted undertaking your education, Francis."

I said nothing to this. His idea of education had been frolics at the Hotel Adlon before ditching me, nearly penniless, in Berlin.

Perhaps he read my mind for he gave me a look, then said, "The boule chest? Genuine ormolu, but the piece is a chimera. They've added the legs from another chest. You might spot that for Philip. He'll be impressed." Then he winked and signaled the waiter for another *pichet de vin blanc*. "To our ventures, Francis. May we find success."

I raised my glass, but I thought that the farther I stayed from my uncle, the better. And lucky for me—or so I thought at the time—a new area of interest opened: the theater. Not Monsieur Armand's little dramas that I was once again finding tedious, but a real theater with real sets and costumes. It was a little avant-garde troupe that, thanks to Madame Dumoulin, had discovered her brother's weird machines and beautiful kites.

"Monsieur Leandres was amazed at the work," she told me when I met her that Thursday. "'So surreal, so beautiful.' He was quite in ecstasies. And even allowing for his melodramatic nature, I could see that he was impressed. Nothing but Jules coming to Paris with a selection of the kites and with the smaller machines to use as models would do. He's almost ready to start work on scaled-up versions of the machines."

"That's wonderful," I said. "Jules is so talented."

Madame nodded. "A step, I think, back to real life. I pray so, Francis."

I glanced at her face. It was a study, as Nan would say, her expression poised between joyful hope and anxiety. "It will be good for him," I said with as much conviction as I could muster, which probably was not enough. After all, who can really predict anything about another person?

"I do believe so. But, Francis, I would feel so much better if you could lend a hand."

"Of course. The machines are fascinating. I could learn so much."

"Ah, I did not mean that, but yes, that would be best. If you would volunteer to help."

I realized then that she wanted me not so much to assist Jules as to keep an eye on him. "Does he have a place to stay in Paris?"

"Not yet."

My new lodging was in the Latin Quarter near the Luxembourg Gardens, and I told her that I thought there was another room available in the same building. If not, there were similar rooms in the area.

"Perfect," said Madame Dumoulin. She invited me for dinner that night, and I promised to help Jules move his work to the city in the morning.

That was how I became involved with Les Mortes Immortels.

They were, as Jules explained to me on the train, surrealist, avant-garde, totally mad. "Just right for my work, don't you think?"

"Your work is terrific. To get it seen—even in a weird performance—can only do you good."

He gave me a look. Jules, I saw, was of two minds. He was thrilled to be at work in Paris; nothing could better signal his recovery. At the same time, I understood that his various projects were undertaken without any thought of selling or even showing them and that, indeed, revealing such intimate things to the world might be disturbing. As usual, what had seemed a simple favor to a friend now threatened to get me into deep water. I decided to stay in the shallows. "Do they have a workshop? Or are you going to have to make everything back home?"

"They claim the theater has a workspace. But we must have a look."

"I'd like to see it," I said, and just like that I committed myself to Les Mortes Immortels, led by Monsieur Pierre Leandres, impresario, director, and playwright. He dressed all in black with a red neck scarf and wore a beret even shabbier than my uncle's. A tall, lean chain-smoker with a fine head of dark hair, a beaky face, and a volatile temper, he drove the whole enterprise, propelled by an intense belief in himself. I was to be impressed by that if not by the work.

Jeanne Berger was the principal female performer. She was short and dark with dyed auburn hair, a hoarse but expressive voice, and the face of an aging fortune-teller. I suspected that her lack of glamour had kept her from better roles in the theater and film, for she was clearly head and shoulders above the rest of the cast in talent and experience, especially the male lead, Marc Boudin. He was very young, very serious, very stupid, but fine-looking in the blond and strapping manner I'd admired in Germany. Besides a wide chest and beautiful legs, his main asset was his voice. When he wasn't warbling the odd, dissonant lyrics and shouting his lines, he sang popular songs with what sounded like real talent, even to my tone-deaf ears.

The ingénue was Catherine Oury. I found her sympathetic. Like me, she was on the run from convention and schooling, having escaped from what she always referred to as the Finishing School from Hell, an establishment in Switzerland with *le cuisine tres horrible* and *les rules tres béte*. Clever and free-spirited, she owed her present freedom to Monsieur Leandres, who had somehow secured her release and who assured her at every turn that the theater was her destiny. I wondered about that, though she clearly enjoyed drama on—and off—stage.

Three young men, Messieurs Duguay, LePage, and Terrien, rounded out the troupe. They played multiple roles, shifted scenery, and swept the stage. In between times, they had long and intense discussions about the meaning of various scenes, the utility of acting, and the possibility of reaching "the masses" who, I guessed, would far rather see Barbette or Josephine Baker. So would I.

"Is there any plot?" I asked Jules. This was about a week into rehearsals, for only the setting, a nightmare industrial landscape, was at all clear.

He stopped sawing the piece of plywood he was shaping.

"Mademoiselle Oury is Human Hope," he said.

"Ah."

"Miscast, of course."

I was a little surprised. Given Jules's affection for actresses, I thought that pretty and lively Catherine Oury would be a favorite.

"She lacks the needed purity of intention," he remarked. "She will not be a success."

Purity of intention seemed a lot to ask of anyone at our age, though I admit she seemed pert and clever rather than imaginative. "And Mademoiselle Berger?"

"Represents the Voice of the Earth, the wisdom of the ages."

"I can see she's had some experience." I guessed she was forty or maybe fifty.

"She deserves better lines," Jules said. "The rest have the speeches they deserve. But that's the point: Life is absurd."

Agreed. And maybe that's what inspired the many squabbles of the cast, who debated every detail and hashed over the meaning of each word. Jules worked away impassively in the storage space behind the stage, scaling up two of his machines. When he was finished, the towering constructions cast enormous shadows over the actors and added a genuinely sinister note to the production.

I was impressed and Jules was pleased. "It is just as I'd imagined," he said.

I regretted the loss of the fine camera I'd had in Berlin. "We must get some photographs."

Jules only shrugged, but Monsieur Leandres saw the potential right away, and over the next days, press photographers arrived to document "the groundbreaking scenery for the latest production of Les Mortes Immortels." As a result, we had a very decent opening-night audience. I know that because I had been enlisted to work one of the machines. As Jules pointed out, motors large enough to move the equipment would drown out the actors.

After listening to many rehearsals, I thought that would not be such a bad thing.

"Yet the machines must move," Jules insisted, "to create the shadows."

I could see that, so on opening night, I sat in a little curtained alcove working the levers that raised and lowered the "hammer" pounding the man-shaped pegs into their holes. This proved trickier than you might think, since the blows were supposed to punctuate the fevered speeches onstage. As the night wore on, my compartment got hotter, and the stage dust found its way into my lungs, causing me to wheeze loudly. But what might have been an embarrassing distraction went quite unnoticed in what became a general uproar.

Thanks to a liberal papering of the house, friends cheered even Monsieur Leandres's most opaque speeches. Ordinary ticket holders were not so charitable, and some booed even the competent Mademoiselle Berger. Defenders took issue with critics and vice versa and soon scuffles broke out, with the audience pushing and shoving, stamping their feet, and clattering over chairs. The actors carried on bravely until a variety of missiles began landing on the stage, whereupon Pierre signaled for the curtain to come down. This was met by applause and jeers in almost equal amounts, before someone began shouting, "*Vive les machines.*"

This chant was taken up so enthusiastically that the curtain was raised again and the spotlight switched on. Jules and I began frantically working our levers and pulleys to such applause that we were ordered to step out and take a bow before the curtain was brought down for the final time. Jules was a bit shaken, I was gasping, and the actors were all drenched in sweat, their greasepaint running and the ladies' wigs askew.

Everyone was stunned except for Pierre, who kept proclaiming that all was *"Merveilleuse!"* and the best production of Les Mortes Immortels ever. "Such a response! Such a controversy! The press coverage will be extensive! Our run extended! Our fame"—he was generous enough to include us all—"secured!"

And he was right. If a mediocre playwright, Pierre Leandres was a first-rate impresario. There were photos in the dailies, discussions in the cafés, lines at the small box office. We had achieved a *succès de scandale*, particularly Jules, who was invited here and there to give his opinions and to show his models and to have his photo taken with this intellectual or that starlet. Now his little—and not so little—oddities were evidence of deep thought and deeper creativity; he was dubbed "the unconscious surrealist" and "the surrealist in spite of himself" and was halfway to being a public figure before he knew it.

Madame Dumoulin worried a little about this, but Jules seemed quite unchanged to me. I assured his sister that he was keeping regular hours and working away as usual. No, it was the younger members of the troupe who had their heads turned. The handsome Marc Boudin was collected every night after the performance by a fine chauffeured limousine. The cast was divided over whether its owner was a countess or merely rich. The three supporting roles gave interviews and swanned around the cafés with impressionable girls, but it was Mademoiselle Oury who was most affected—and who really caused the trouble.

Not that I blamed her. She'd switched the Finishing School from Hell for the glamour of the theater and a grown-up lover. I could see that in theory. In practice, I knew grown-up lovers tended to be difficult and, on closer acquaintance, Les Mortes Immortels was definitely short on glamour. For a few nights, even a few weeks, the glow could be sustained. After that, reality set in. As Human Hope, poor Catherine had a good deal of standing about, making her a favorite target not only for hostile critics but for the disgruntled patrons (and outright troublemakers) who turned up with bits of fruit and wads of paper and other missiles. The occasional bottle landed onstage, too, and after she cut her foot one night (Human Hope was, of course, barefoot) she had a set-to with Pierre, complete with shouting, cursing, tears, broken glass, and a ripped costume. Afterward, Pierre took her out for a late-night supper and plied her with champagne and flattery to no avail.

As I approached the theater the next afternoon, I saw her waiting a block away. She looked charming dressed in her gray schoolgirl blazer, boater hat, and navy skirt, and she came right to the point. "I'm running away, Francis."

I secretly thought that a good idea: She was no actress. "Who's going to do Human Hope?"

"I don't know and I don't care. Will you tell Pierre I've gone to Brussels?"

"Of course. Is that where you are going?"

She gave a sly smile. "Actually, no. South of France, but he doesn't need to know that. Or with whom. I'm going to lie in the sun and be adored instead of being a target for half the oafs in Paris."

"That sounds good," I said.

"But tell him Brussels. He'll make a fuss. *Tant pis.*"

With this, she leaned over, kissed my cheek, and skipped away, light and careless, leaving behind a crisis in the theater and a full-blown tantrum from our director. Mademoiselle Berger saved the day by calling in her niece, a skinny and diminutive waif who suggested, as Jules put it, the feebleness of all our hopes. Surprisingly, he was the one who solved this little problem for us—and landed me in a real mess.

CHAPTER FIVE

Dear Nan,

I'm learning more about the theater. For one thing, the cardinal rule really is that the show must go on. And now I can tell you that it will, because Jules arrived yesterday afternoon with a new Human Hope. Her name is Mademoiselle Inessa, and she was apparently too big of a star back in the Soviet Union to need any surname. I believe that—she is a sensation.

Absolutely true. We'd assembled in the theater for a cast meeting, the actors all very glum about Mademoiselle Oury's defection. Pierre had just demanded to know where Jules was, and what we were going to do to find a real Human Hope, when the door opened and Jules led in the most beautiful woman I'd ever seen. She was tall and slender with a head of white-blond hair, cut short to reveal a long white neck. She had very large, wide-set gray eyes and a beautiful sculptured mouth and nose set in a broad and perfectly symmetrical face. "C'est Mademoiselle Inessa," Jules said. "Our Human Hope."

> *The men of the cast have fallen at her feet, and Monsieur Leandres has been rewriting scenes and altering dialogue because she knows little French. Though, previously, every word in the play was sacred, now he finds no difficulty cutting whole paragraphs. Probably a good thing. I'll admit that a glance at her makes me feel more hopeful, and I suspect that a shorter play can only be an improvement.*

So it was. In my next letter, I was able to report that our run, due to end as soon as the scandal of the opening subsided, was now to be extended well beyond our even optimistic director's hopes. Les Mortes Immortels enjoyed another big surge in publicity thanks to Inessa. She was "so charmed to be in Paris." "The language, yes, it made difficulties." But her role, very small, was "just right to get her started performing en français." It was "the dream of her life" to act before the Parisian audience. To share her art with the oh-so-receptive French. I can quote Inessa because she said the same things every time she was interviewed, Jules having helped her memorize suitable answers. Though shy and wary, Inessa was quick and she had a good ear; what little she could say, she pronounced perfectly. But perhaps because I was less dazed than the other men, I began to doubt both her acting ability and her experience, even though she was marvelous as Human Hope. She stood center stage looking radiant and hearts melted. Instead of week-old fruit, the audience now threw single roses and daisies and bouquets of lilies, crackling in their protective paper.

Just the same, I couldn't help noticing that Inessa seemed puzzled by the blocking and had to be led through every bit of stage business. One evening, I hung around until I could leave the theater with Mademoiselle Berger. I liked the older actress's age-battered face and her voice, cured with cigarettes and cognac.

"*Eh, bien*, Francis," she said. "What do you think of our play now?"

"I still think you deserve better, Mademoiselle."

She laughed. "The theater is a cruel master. The audience is capricious, directors unfair, and playwrights mediocre. But you are safe, no? You have no desire for the limelight."

"None whatsoever."

"Fortunate boy." But here she looked at me more closely. "Yet you are working all day for Monsieur Armand and then coming to the theater for the machine."

"A favor to Jules. His older sister has been most kind to me."

"Jules is a wounded soul," she observed.

"At last recovering. But he could not work both machines. And learning construction skills will be invaluable for me."

"A young man of good sense."

I thought that a man of any sense would avoid avant-garde theater. "I wanted to ask you about Inessa."

Now her expression, which had been tired and genial, her after-performance look, became sharp and interested.

"Do you think she was ever onstage before?"

"You mean, do I believe that she was a famous actress in old Russia or somewhere else to the east?"

I nodded.

"No—at least not on the stage. Film?" She pursed her lips and shrugged. "Maybe film, because the camera loves her. Even her press photos are magical."

"I saw a lot of Russian films in Berlin and many German productions, too. I know I would have remembered her face."

"Exaggerating one's credits is not unheard of in our profession. But to be able to stand onstage virtually speechless as Human Hope"—here Mademoiselle gave a throaty laugh—"and not get booed off the boards, that is a gift of the theatrical deities. Too bad that the talkies are threatening. She has a face for the screen but not yet a voice."

"I think she may be a wounded soul, too," I said, for even without words, Inessa projected a variety of emotions, all grounded by what might have been fear or sorrow.

Mademoiselle Berger nodded. "Ah, perhaps that is why she and the eccentric Jules are now such friends."

"Jules is a romantic."

"Well, he has found himself a true *belle dame*, a woman of mystery, *comme Cendrillon*."

"Let us hope she is not *sans merci*," I said.

We had reached the nearby Metro, and Mademoiselle Berger stopped to light a cigarette before saying good night. I could see that her only concern was that interest in our mysterious Inessa should keep the troupe employed. I was in a different situation, having promised Madame Dumoulin I'd watch out for Jules.

Building the machines and working them in performance and being admired were all good for him, but I was beginning to worry that Inessa might be another matter.

Jules had been safe enough dreaming of his favorite entertainers, pasting their pictures in his scrapbooks and painting them on his kites. Now a genuine star had landed on his particular piece of earth, and he was entranced. He was with her as often as he could manage, and where Inessa was concerned, he showed a good deal of ingenuity. Nearly every afternoon, she had interviews and photo sessions, and Jules was her interpreter, her guide around Paris, her protector from overeager journalists and columnists.

Come evening, they were at the theater. At the last possible minute, Jules stuck his head in her dressing room to wish her luck. He was always out of his machine in time to kiss her hand and to congratulate her after every performance. I could see that she trusted him and enjoyed his attentions, but as far as I could tell, she remained safe on her pedestal, or perhaps in her pumpkin, for Mademoiselle Berger's reference to Cinderella was apt. As soon as the final curtain came down, Inessa threw her coat over her costume, stuck her feet into a pair of pumps, and without even removing her stage makeup, clattered down to the alley and into the cab that was invariably waiting for her.

Who was inside? I skipped my bow one night and went straight out. The cab was already there. I pretended a great and absentminded rush, and I had the door open before the cabbie could protest that it was *occupé*. A tough-looking fellow in a rumpled jacket and a soft cap sat in the rear seat. He did not look flush enough to hire a cab, never mind to keep the meter running while Mademoiselle Inessa finished her curtain calls. His cap and the dark interior hid his eyes, but I caught a glimpse of a strong unshaven jaw and wide, thin lips.

My heart jumped; the clothes, the jaw, and something about his rawboned frame reminded me strongly of both the lethal Igor and one of the Cossacks I'd seen near the Beehive. "*Excusez-moi!*" I drew back in the hope I would not be recognized.

"This cab is taken," he said. His French was heavily accented, and the accent was Russian. I apologized again and shut the door, just as Mademoiselle Inessa hurried from the theater. She gave me a wild, almost imploring look, then slipped inside. The cabbie immediately put the taxi in gear and pulled away.

"Who is he?" I asked Jules the first time I managed to speak to him alone.

"Who is who?"

"The man who collects Inessa every night after the performance."

"That's Alexi. Inessa's brother."

"Her brother?" Their appearance, manners, even her excellent accent and his coarse speech all told against this. He looked like a street thug; she looked like a princess. I couldn't believe they were related, and I wondered if Jules did—or if he just wanted to.

"Much older," he continued quickly. "Very protective. The rest of the family was killed or exiled, which amounted to much the same thing at the time. Of course, their money was gone and their assets appropriated, so there were all kinds of difficulties leaving the Soviet Union. Alexi managed to get her out via Istanbul."

"She couldn't have done much theatrical work in those conditions, could she?"

"I believe that she was onstage as a child. No matter how bad the conditions, there was always theater. Aristocrat or commissar, there's always someone who can pay."

I saw he was so completely enthralled that logic, even plausibility, had gone out the window. My erotic life being much less elevated, I found it hard to imagine his state of mind or to decide if merging lust and love in such a way would be desirable. And what about Inessa, whose heart was a closed book? I began trying to make conversation with her, but although I could see that she understood well enough, she responded only in the rote phrases that Jules had taught her would be acceptable for the press.

"She feels safe that way," he explained. "So many people want her to do this or that. Want her to say something interesting or shocking. Want to know her politics." He sniffed. "I think Inessa would be happy never to hear of politics again: Red, white, Communist, Socialist, capitalist, czarist. All the same."

"And the brother?"

"It's not surprising that he has some rough edges. He was old enough to see action toward the end of the war, and he fought later near Odessa."

My thought was that more likely he was a gangster first to last. "It must be hard for them—financially, I mean."

"Inessa has patrons willing to take a chance on her future and help her now."

I wondered if that included Jules himself and guessed it probably did. Still, to be out in the world and feted for his work had to be a boost for him. Madame Dumoulin, who shared my anxieties, said that helping the young actress might be a good thing. "One forgets one's own sorrows in someone else's," she said, as if she'd had experience along those lines.

Besides, I had plenty to do with the machines and being the apprentice and charming Philip and enjoying the excitements of Paris. I'd have continued to mind my own business if I had not arrived at the theater one evening to hear Inessa say, ". . . hours and hours AND HOURS with Monsieur Matisse. I am exhausted."

Matisse! One of the art gods of the moment. "You've met Matisse?" I asked, deeply envious.

She turned around and saw me. "*Bien sure!* Francis. This is the second time I pose. First time, not so bad. He takes a brush and black ink and—" She swept her arm in the air, expressive hands, flexible wrist, to show how the artist had covered a big sheet of paper. "There I am! *Tres jolie.*" A big smile.

This was more animation than Inessa had showed me before. "You have been honored. Matisse is a great artist."

"Of course," she said. "Without question. But today was a portrait in oils. I am sitting still for hours in the smell of the—what is it?"

"Turpentine. It is used to thin the paints and clean the brushes."

"It gives me the headache," Inessa said. "I thought in Paris one dances and sings and enjoys life. In Paris, I sit all morning for painters, breathing up poisons and ruining my complexion. At night, I stand onstage and look to the heavens. I am forever tiring my derriere or my legs. I want to dance!"

She took a nimble-footed twirl around the stage, provoking Jules to whistle one of the dance numbers so popular in the cabarets and dance halls. He held out his arms, and Inessa, already swaying to the tune, joined him to circle the stage in a lively foxtrot.

"Keep the beat, Francis," she called and broke off to snap her fingers until I began to clap in time. Around and around they went before she stopped and said, "Whistle me a Charleston."

"I can't dance and whistle," Jules said, laughing. But he found enough air to pipe up a jazzy American number. Inessa took center stage alone, raised her arms, and calling, "Clap, Francis," launched into an enthusiastic Charleston, hair bouncing, feet flying, her face radiant. She continued until Jules ran out of air, and I lost the beat.

"Oh," she said, laughing. "I need the jazz band and the Negro musicians."

"Instead," I said, "you have painters."

"A dozen at least," she said, joking, though a little shadow came over her happy face. "I must not talk of them," she added quickly, "but I would trade them all for a dance band." She snapped her fingers again in a jazzy rhythm and moved gaily across the floor.

I thought that this was the real Inessa, not the timid and nearly speechless Human Hope or the press sensation with her memorized phrases. I was enjoying her carefree dancing and thinking that she might indeed have a future as an entertainer, before her phrase "a dozen painters" registered. That one or two might have seen the play and admired Human Hope was not unimaginable. A dozen was another matter entirely. I had a memory of my now-French uncle opening his notebook to write down the names of painters, and saying, "Stick with the gilt-edged ones, my boy."

It wasn't possible that there was a connection. What did my uncle know about art but what I'd told him? And how could the seedy-looking Claude convince not one but a dozen painters to tackle a portrait—almost certainly for free? It was ridiculous. My fondness for Jules and my anxiety about his unsettled mind had set my own imagination loose.

I looked at Inessa and Jules, dancing a slow waltz this time, happy for the moment in spite of her thuggish brother and the precarious life of Les Mortes Immortels and his wounds. But this time there was no lift in my heart. My uncle Lastings, in whatever disguise, existed on the improbable. As he told me in Berlin when I questioned a phony aid organization: *It could have been real.* My uncle Lastings could imagine whatever would bring him profit.

It wasn't likely, of course it wasn't, but I couldn't shake the feeling that my now-French uncle had entangled Inessa in one of his schemes. That could be dangerous for her, and if I was right about the thuggish Alexi, dangerous for Jules and for my uncle, as well.

CHAPTER SIX

Philip liked to play at being jealous. I like older men, I really do, but I find them complicated. My taste is for sex plain and simple—well, maybe not *entirely* simple—but I can do without the drama, the make-believe, the heavy emotions. When it comes right down to it, I trust the body more than the mind.

But Philip, as I said, liked to play at being jealous, which complicated my attempts to locate my uncle. Perhaps I should just have trolled the Dôme, Le Select, or, more likely yet, the Parnasse Bar with its demi-celebrity barman. But after seeing Alexi, Inessa's supposed brother, I preferred the indirect approach. "Are we going to go look at that boule chest, Philip?" I asked one night.

We were having an after-theater supper. Philip thought the play was rubbish, but he was thrilled to be connected to a theatrical sensation, and yours truly was thereby elevated from pickup to trophy. I was now always introduced not as, "Francis, who's studying design," but as "Francis—with Les Mortes Immortels. He works one of the machines, don't you know." This provided an opening for a discussion of the play—impenetrable—and of the machines—formidable—and Philip was sure to put in that "Francis worked closely with the set designer, too, and helped scale up the models." From being only a step up from a rent boy, I was now on my way to artistic lion.

Though I thought it would be a good idea if Claude was contacted by my friend Philip, he was having none of it. "Oh, I think not. Not with your present celebrity. Old Claude has an eye for a pretty boy. And especially a pretty boy with talent!" He gave me a roguish look and squeezed my knee.

"What would a boule chest be worth in London?" I asked, hoping to distract him, because I knew quite well what he wanted: a jealous scene that would end with my leaving in a temper—most unfortunate as we had not consumed the promised *mousse au chocolat* that I had spotted on the dessert trolley—followed by frantic apologies from Philip and concluding with reconciliation in his big bed at the Hotel George V. If I had my way, I'd have gone right to the hotel and enjoyed myself before ordering up a *mousse au chocolat* from room service.

Now Philip frowned. "Quite a bit. For the right customer. The Right Honorable—" He caught himself at the last moment. He did love dropping names, a habit at odds with a dealer's necessary discretion. His compromise was to mention titles only or give a description focused on the client's possessions, as *A lady I've dealt with for years. Sèvres porcelain, my dear, famille rose by preference; she simply can't get enough of it,* accompanied by a smirk and a titter. "The Right Honorable loves ormolu. But it has to be the real thing."

I asked about this distinction.

"Done by mercury plating. That's the real ormolu, and it's marvelous, gives a satin coating like no other. The French government outlawed the process early in the last century. Why? My dear, it was so toxic the workers took ill and died, but the plating was superb."

Though it sounded appalling, I said that I'd like to see some of it. Philip's face grew stiff, but I'd known him long enough to spot the twinkle in his eye.

"You young rascal, you fancy Claude! A bit rough and too long in the tooth for my taste, but for the undiscerning—"

I saw there was nothing for it. I protested loudly enough and long enough to arouse real suspicion. The little scene culminated when I threw down my napkin and, with a regretful glance at the dessert trolley and an apologetic shrug for the maître d', stormed out of the restaurant. Once on the street, I looked about for a little park or Metro stop or somewhere convenient for Philip's semitearful apology. I had the routine down pat.

Late that night at the George V, I judged the time was right. "I really should see a genuine example of ormolu. To complete my education."

"Certainly, Francis," Philip said, finishing the last of his champagne—our quarrels tended to end with champagne. "I'll give Claude a ring. Mind you, I'm not sure I'll buy anything from him. I suspect he's a bit of a bounder."

I could only add amen to that.

The next afternoon, though, we arrived at a little close off the boulevard Saint-Germain, a rather better address than I'd expected. The main building was a respectable town house; the stable behind had been converted to a showroom, probably with an attached workspace, for there was a strong smell of thinner and oil paint.

Claude met us at the door wearing a gray worker's smock as if he'd just been polishing up the stock or doing some refinishing. He seemed momentarily surprised by customers but quickly switched into full dealer mode. "Welcome, Philip! And Francis, isn't it? Come in. We're in dishabille at the moment, what with moving in. I have a few choice things. Choice as you'll see. Though for you, Philip, only the boule chest will do."

That item was standing by itself, plump, shiny, and curvaceous with the famous—and to my mind, sinister—ormolu running up its legs like decorated stockings on a showgirl. It was certainly a fancy piece, and Philip did it justice, poring over it like a surgeon with a tricky op to prepare and pointing out the beauties of the inlay and the sheen of the metalwork.

I feigned an interest I didn't possess and slid away as soon as I could to look at the other pieces, chairs and tables mostly. I didn't need an expert eye to see that they were vastly inferior to the boule chest that Claude and Philip were attempting to date. Philip thought post-1830, and Claude, quite naturally, was holding out for a date before the 1830 mercury process prohibition. I guessed that my uncle had purchased a load of cheap goods, then added the one genuinely valuable piece to lend luster to the rest.

I worked my way through a thicket of chairs until I spotted a doorway open just a crack. The source of the paint smell? I glanced behind me. Philip had commenced what looked to be

serious negotiations for the chest, and Claude was occupied. I
eased the door open. Inside were two big open racks filled with
canvases. From the smell, they were still drying. And the subject
matter? I took a step inside but, as always, my uncle was watching his perimeter.

"*C'est privé!*" called Claude, who wasn't pleased at all.

"*Je suis désolé*," I said, but not before I'd caught a glimpse of
a woman's face done in Matisse's bold purples, reds, and blues.
Could that swath of creamy white be Inessa's fair hair? I thought
so, though at a quick glimpse I couldn't be sure. "Your paintings
are as interesting as your furniture. I couldn't resist a look."

Despite this apology, he hustled over and locked the door,
while Philip, who likes to show off his expertise, began discussing paintings as commodity. "Much more difficult to move," he
said. "Horse and hounds, stately homes and fine landscapes—I
will take a flyer on those if the frames are good. Ancestor portraits? Your nouveau riche will sometimes go for a noble face to
put over a mantelpiece. Sometimes."

"The paintings are not my stock," Claude said. "I share the space
with an art dealer. It's a minor collection being stored until it can be
shipped off to—the Argentine, was it? Or was it to be Shanghai?"
He twisted his mouth to indicate indifference. "No matter."

I got a dark look, and I changed subject to the chest. "Are the
legs the same type of wood?" I asked.

"Well, now," said Philip. "They are. They certainly are, but
are they the original legs of this piece? That's the question."

This occupied them for several minutes, during which time
Claude got out his Gauloises and lit a cigarette. The matches

were from the Parnasse Bar. He gave me another look, and I nodded. Then he and Philip got serious about the price for the chest, negotiations that ended with handshakes all around. I thought perhaps I would be dispatched to pick up the chest, but no. I had to give my uncle high marks for thoroughness. He had access to a van and would deliver the chest. Or ship it, if Philip preferred.

"Oh, we'll have it shipped." He took out his London card and arranged for the chest to be wrapped like a baby and well insured. On our return from Claude's shop, Philip was in fine form. Whatever it was in Paris, in London, the chest would certainly be pre-1830 and all of a piece and at least 50 percent more expensive. On the strength of this we had a celebratory dinner that saw us both in a fine mood. Philip, because he had done a good bit of business, and I, because I now knew how to contact my uncle.

Just the same, it was several days before the stars aligned, and I managed an early evening visit to the Parnasse Bar without Philip. He didn't know that I'd been excused from the machine for the night. Our run in Paris was at last nearing an end, but there was talk of taking what its author was now calling a "Surrealist Entertainment" on the road. I had no intention of leaving Paris, so Les Mortes Immortels were breaking in another operator.

At the Parnasse, I ordered a *vin blanc* and asked the indispensable Jimmy whether Claude was around. He indicated patience and, at a momentary lull, disappeared into the back. My uncle arrived within half an hour. He ordered a whiskey and tipped Jimmy well.

"I didn't expect to see you again, my boy."

"I felt you were owed a warning."

"About what, *mon vieux*?" Even when we were speaking English, my uncle liked to sprinkle in some French phrases.

"I need to know if you are involved in some way with Inessa. Our theater's star Human Hope."

He raised his eyebrows. I should say that my uncle rarely gets the wind up. "Inessa is a talent. Quite genuine, you know."

"Inessa is remarkable, but she's no actress. You must know that."

"Neither was Helen of Troy, though she had a face that launched a thousand ships."

"What about a few dozen paintings? In the back room of your shop? Behind that locked door? I'm guessing those are portraits of Inessa."

He didn't respond right away, and I added, "I know she's sat twice for Matisse. How you managed that I can't imagine."

"You underestimate me. One look at her and they were tripping over their easels. All except the little Spanish bastard. A surprise, that. He's supposed to be death to women."

"Picasso! You approached Picasso, too." I thought that my uncle might at least have taken me with him.

"I followed your list, my boy. And very useful it was."

"You might have let me see the paintings," I said.

"Alas, they are still under wraps, only to be revealed at our show, *A Tribute of Talent to Beauty*." He whipped out a little brochure, written in the high-flown style I remembered from the racket he ran in Weimar. "*Introducing a young actress of exceptional talent to the French public*."

"And who profits from all this?"

He feigned offense. "You should have been put to the law, Francis. You have, I fear, a legalistic and suspicious mind. Our project is totally legitimate, though, of course, expenses must be covered. We are entrepreneurs and impresarios. And you—or at least your theatrical friends—have already profited, haven't you? Would that ridiculous production still be ongoing without her? Not a chance. As for Inessa, she is being launched on a major theatrical career."

As usual, I could see that my uncle half believed his own scam.

"She has no experience," I said. "And her French—"

"Her French is better than you think. Timing was important, and a delay, supposedly to improve her language, proved ideal."

"Nonetheless, she is completely untrained. She has to be led by the hand through any blocking. What happens if she does get a big part?"

"She'll sink or swim, my boy. You're not the only one who can negotiate a tough spot. Believe me, she won't turn down an opportunity for fame and fortune."

Maybe not. I'd seen a different Inessa the day she complained about the portrait sittings and danced with Jules. "What about Alexi?" I asked. "Her 'brother.'"

My uncle's face, up to then complacent, turned serious. "There I have a tiger by the tail," he admitted.

I felt a pang for Jules; things were as I'd guessed. "Is he really her brother?"

My uncle had perfected the Gallic shrug. "He could be her brother. It's not impossible," he said.

"But unlikely."

"Oh, highly."

"Though he is ex-military and fought in the civil war?"

"That is for certain. It's probably how he acquired Inessa."

I must have looked surprised.

"A cultivated young woman, educated, French speaking—you can tell, can't you, that her accent is excellent? How does she wind up with a thug like Alexi but through the fortunes of war and revolution? The Bolsheviks stripped the nobility of their land, money, and possessions, then killed or exiled them. So-called enemies of the people were for the chop whether they were filthy rich or desperately poor, admirable citizens or bloodsucking exploiters. A teenage girl alone with Inessa's extraordinary looks would probably have landed in a brothel in Shanghai or Istanbul. You can be thankful that Alexi had more imagination than to turn her immediately to cash."

My uncle frowned, lit another cigarette, and continued. "He was probably her best ticket to survival. Though I could wish she had selected someone more amenable. Even someone with a sense of the ridiculous would be an improvement."

"He picks her up in a taxi immediately after each performance."

"Don't I know it. He sends me the bills."

So my uncle was financing the upfront costs. And how would he recoup them? *A Tribute of Talent to Beauty* at some gallery? No chance. This was a swindle for sure, and someone was going to wind up the loser. "It's not just him you have to worry about. I'm sure I've seen him with the tough Russian group that hangs around the old Beehive. They are revolutionary exiles of one persuasion or another, and if he's involved with them, you and Inessa and—other friends—are in danger."

He clapped me on the shoulder. "A concern that does you credit, my boy. But all is tickety-boo at the moment. Though"— and here Claude did seem a great deal like old familiar Uncle Lastings, quick to see every angle and eager for an exit strategy— "there may come a time when you can lend a hand."

Oh, no! I'd been down that road before and it led to nowhere good. "I wanted to warn you. I do not want to get involved in another dodgy scheme."

"Dodgy! This is culture, my boy, and French culture at that. Great painters, a great and talented beauty. All that remains is to hire the hall so to speak."

"I'm glad to hear it, but Alexi's part of a bad crowd."

"Know that for a fact, do you?" His expression was keen and interested.

"Let's say I've seen enough of them to do me."

"We're wrapping up soon," he said, and for the first time I thought he looked not just serious but worried. "A delicate time. But I have good cards to play, so into the breach!"

My heart sank. He'd almost convinced me that he had every- thing in hand and a plan for every eventuality, but it's a sure sign of trouble when Uncle Lastings turns to military metaphors. I assumed that the same held true for Claude, and that night I waited for Jules after the performance, time I spent pacing back and forth and considering one course of action then another.

Although I didn't feel I owed my uncle very much, I didn't want to endanger him unnecessarily. On the other hand, I not only liked Jules, I had also promised his sister I would watch out for him. Then there was Inessa with her beautiful face and her dangerous guardian. What I right about her? Was I right about Alexi? Was Uncle Lastings? What if I was wrong or if Jules didn't believe me? Such thoughts made for an unpleasant evening.

I loitered behind a news and advertising kiosk as it neared time for the performance to end. Right on time, a taxi slowed and parked at the head of the stage door alley across from me. I caught a glimpse of Alexi when his lighter flared for a cigarette. Not five minutes later, Inessa emerged and scrambled into the taxi. I waited until they drove off, then crossed the street and tapped on the stage door.

"*Bon soir*, Francis," said Jacques, the old doorman. He jokingly asked if I already missed my machine. We chatted for a minute or two before I could ask if Jules had left.

"Not yet, not yet," Jacques said. He proceeded to regale me with an account of how the little slips and mishaps of the new operator for my machine had added to the general hilarity of the performance. As our run continued, more and more of the audience had found humor in the piece to our director's distress—and profit.

Shortly, Jules came down with Hector, my replacement. We all shook hands, and I offered to buy them a drink. It was only after we'd talked about the machines and the half-finalized plans for a provincial tour, and Hector had departed, that Jules and I set out for our rooms. "Would you go on the tour if it materializes?" I asked. After much thought, this was the best opening I could manage.

"Depends. I'm not sure Inessa wants to continue."

"Human Hope is not a role with much scope," I agreed. "But has she enough French for a better part?"

"Her French is good. It's always been good. She is not uneducated."

This was an unwelcome confirmation of my uncle's theory. "Yet at first her language seemed very uncertain."

"That was Alexi's idea entirely. To create mystery and build interest."

"Without having her actually perform onstage?"

"Yes. You were always a little suspicious about that, weren't you, Francis?"

We passed beneath a streetlight and, though his tone was resentful, I saw that his face was drawn, his eyes melancholy. As far as I knew, he had not hit a bad patch since he started working with Les Mortes Immortels. That decided me. "I am worried about Inessa with this portrait business, because I've met one of the men involved. He is a scoundrel named Claude Roleau, a part-time antiques dealer. He is apparently in partnership with Alexi. They've amassed a considerable number of portraits from the best contemporary artists. Those works are bound to be valuable."

There was no response from Jules. I decided to let this information sink in.

"They will become more valuable yet if she makes a big theatrical success," he said after a moment, but his tone was thoughtful.

"Very true. But Roleau is not overly patient, and I am guessing that Alexi is not, either. They'll be set to profit whether Inessa gets a good role or not. I suspect that a theatrical career is to be her share. And if she doesn't get one, where will she be then?"

"She has loyal friends."

Now it was my turn to be silent.

After a minute or two, he said, "She will not leave Alexi, though she is half afraid of him. I have already suggested."

Another grim confirmation of Uncle Lastings's theory. "Naturally, she cares about her brother."

"Yes, only natural," he said, but there was a weariness in his voice that told me he did not believe it.

"Get her away from Paris," I said impulsively. "Alexi may be too poor to follow you, because I know for a fact that even the nightly taxi is paid for by his partner. And, Jules, Alexi has other, more dangerous, friends. I've seen him with a bunch of gangster-ish Russian exiles."

"The whole Russian contingent is mourning Mother Russia," Jules observed.

"Inessa, too?"

He shook his head. "Inessa wants to stay in Paris. The thing is, she really does have a brother, a younger brother. They were orphaned when their parents were sentenced to something called 'minus six' and died in exile in Irbit. Alexi was a local Bolshevik functionary, and he took them under his protection. He had a chance to get to the West, but somehow Inessa and Pavel were separated during the trip. Although there's no reason to think so, she's convinced that Pavel's here somewhere, and she's set her heart on finding him."

"Paris isn't going away. She could return when it's safe."

When he hesitated, I said impulsively, "In the meantime, couldn't we make a search for her brother?"

A pause that I took to be a sign he was considering the idea. "Paris is enormous."

"We'd get as much information from Inessa as possible, and if we can't find the boy ourselves—we can hire a detective. There are such people."

Jules stopped and laid his hand on my shoulder. "You are good for me, Francis. I get discouraged sometimes, pursued by *le chien noir*. You make everything sound simple."

"What we need to do *is* simple: get Inessa away from Alexi and his partner. Doing it is what's difficult. We need to make a plan. We need to find an opportunity when she is out of his sight."

"We'll need to convince Inessa, first," he said.

"You do that," I said, as Uncle Lastings's words popped into my mind, "and let me think about an exit strategy."

CHAPTER SEVEN

Inessa wouldn't hear of leaving, although she did not seem at all surprised to learn that Alexi had a dubious partner. "Alexi knows how to survive," she said indifferently. "He will not let himself be cheated."

That was hardly my worry. "There are also his Russian associates, dangerous types."

She made a little face. "Russia is full of dangerous types," she said.

I suspected that was true, but when she added that she had a "duty to the theater," I wondered if she had been infected by our director's pretensions. Or if she was less fond of Jules than she seemed, or, a ghastly thought, more enamored of Alexi than was reasonable. No matter what we said, the only thing that caught her imagination was the notion of a detective. "That is a good idea," she said first in Russian, then in French.

Jules declared that he would find someone for her. "There are agencies," he explained. "Possibly your brother had contact with one of the international relief outfits or with the police.

And certainly he must have an identity card. An investigator will know how to search."

"Whoever we hire will need information," I said. "A photo would be good."

At this, Inessa opened her hands and let them drop. "All gone." She spoke rapidly in Russian in a voice heavy with sorrow. In her native language, her voice seemed lower and more expressive, as if she might really have theatrical talent, developed or not. Jules put his arm around her, and she collected herself. "My brother's name is Pavel, Pavel Lagunov. He would be thirteen now. I last saw him two years ago. Then he was close to my height. Blond with brown eyes and very, very thin and pale. But we were starving at the time. Maybe in Paris, he is plump and rosy. Maybe he is happy, maybe he—"

"Anything distinctive?" Jules interrupted, his face troubled. I could tell that her hopes, so unlikely, gave him pain. "A scar, a birthmark?"

She thought a moment. "He'd had his appendix out. So a scar there. And a birthmark, yes. Small on his left, no, his right shoulder blade. Not too big. The size of a strawberry."

"What about his features," I asked. "Is there a family resemblance?" Which was to my mind the politest way of asking if he was as beautiful as she was.

She immediately shook her head. "Oh, no, Pavel has a face like an angel. *Tres beau!*"

While I wondered if she could really be so oblivious to her own appearance, she continued, "Pavel's very bright and musical. He plays both violin and piano. Maybe he, too, is working in the theater, with music, with people who will protect him." In her distress, she wrung her hands then wiped her eyes.

"And have you been looking for him? You and Alexi?" I asked.

Her faced changed. "Not Alexi. Alexi will never help—and he has his eye on me always. He would rather never see Pavel again. It is Alexi who left him behind. It is Alexi who did not pay for a second ticket. 'He will be on the ship,' he promised me. 'It is not safe to go all together.' When we were at sea, I learned the truth, that I might be of use to him, but Pavel might grow to be a danger. That was his thought, though he pretended it was all an accident."

Inessa struggled to control herself, and Jules took her hand. She gave him a weak smile. "When we were hungry and homeless, Pavel and me, we used to joke that if we were separated, we'd meet in Paris. Now here I am. If Pavel is alive, he is here or he will come. I must stay."

"Your name has been in the newspapers and magazines," I suggested. "And on posters. Wouldn't he have noticed, if he is here?"

She shook her head. "It is such a small show. And poor Pavel did not have as much education as me, not with the war and then the revolution. I doubt he can read French, though he speaks it, yes. We had a French governess." She took a turn around the room before crying, "He might be here! He must be here! He is changed, I know it, just as I am changed. We are not in rags and starving and bones front and back. We might miss each other on the street or pass each other by on the Metro! I'm so afraid that will happen. I cannot leave without finding him."

"There are dangers in staying," I suggested.

She straightened her back, a habitual gesture. "I am used to danger and I can manage Alexi. But a detective! That is a good idea."

"How do you select a detective?" Jules asked me later. We were standing in the little alcove that held our local *tabac*'s phone with the directory open to *agences de détective*. Jules was poring over the listings. "'Matrimonial Our Specialty.' I do not think we need matrimonial."

"That will be divorces."

"Infidelity seems to be keeping a lot of detectives employed," he remarked.

"If only we knew for certain that Pavel *had* entered the country. Then we could try the records of the various relief agencies. And we could be sure a French investigator is what we need."

"My sister volunteered for a refugee assistance group during the war," Jules said. "I think she keeps in touch with some of the other workers. I will ask her if she knows anyone who still works with refugees."

"That's good," I said. "And a detective?"

Jules tapped one of the entries. "'Twenty years' experience with the Paris Préfecture. Missing Persons, Matrimonial, Industrial.' That covers the ground, don't you think?"

"I like that 'Missing Persons' is first on the list."

"Most likely lovers on the lam or runaway husbands or wives. But, yes," Jules said. "I think we should talk to this Monsieur Chaput."

• • •

We went the next morning. Inessa was sitting again for her oil portrait, and in any case, she didn't want Alexi to know about our plan. He had spells of being intensely busy, she said. Periods of late, late nights, mysterious errands, and even more mysterious calls and messages. At those times, he was irritable and unreasonable. Then, as suddenly as it had arrived, his mood would lift. "Then," she said, "he can be charming. Then he brings flowers and chocolates and pretty clothes." She shrugged. "I think he may be working for the commissars still."

That was an unpleasant thought, and remembering Igor and the bad night in the Montparnasse cemetery, I wondered just what Alexi's work entailed. Inessa had no further information: "About his work, about how he earns the money we live on?" She drew her hand across her lips. "Not a peep."

I suspected that we would not get very far asking Alexi about Pavel Lagunov.

So the next morning, Jules and I climbed the steep, dark stair to a fourth-floor office on the rue Clovis. The building was old, and the dust was older. I was wheezing by the second floor and sneezing by the fourth. Monsieur Sylvan Chaput resided behind a door emblazoned with AGENCE DE DÉTECTIVE in faded gold-and-black letters. The office appeared dark. Jules and I exchanged a glance then tried the door. It opened into a waiting room furnished with a pair of wooden chairs and a rickety table holding two newspapers from the day before. The single bare bulb high overhead remained unlit.

Jules cleared his throat, and the inner door opened immediately. "*Bonjour, messieurs,*" said the proprietor, a wiry figure with a dark, seamed face, black eyes, and a fine hawk nose. He looked too small to have been a member of any police force anywhere, but he was spry and alert, and he gave us a comprehensive look as he shook our hands.

"*Entre, s'il vous plait.*" He ushered us into his office, as spare as the waiting room and as shabby as the hallway, but equipped with a row of good solid file cabinets. The large desk held stacks of paper on one side, a green glass shaded lamp and a telephone on the other. Monsieur Chaput gestured toward two chairs and sat down himself. His desk chair must have been quite a tall one, because once behind the desk he appeared of average or more than average height.

After he wrote down Pavel's name, age, and description, he asked, "Possible date of entry?"

"His sister arrived in June two years ago. Pavel could not have entered France much earlier."

"Very good. We have a window, *messieurs*. About two years. These cases," and he tapped the desk for emphasis, "are usually solved in the documents. And the documents are many. The bureaucrat, he likes paper, eh? He lives on paper like the petite book louse."

We agreed with this, though I was a little bit disappointed. Light reading had led me to imagine Monsieur Chaput would be an entertaining combination of Sherlock Holmes and Bulldog Drummond. Clearly, our detective was more at home trolling the archives and pestering their keepers than venturing out with cries of "The game's afoot."

"We must establish some things first, *messieurs*. Did Monsieur

Pavel Lagunov enter France? That is number one and most important. If he is not here . . ."—he raised his hands expressively— "Nothing is impossible, but that would make major complications."

We agreed with that. It was a long way from anywhere in the Workers' Paradise to Paris and there were many possible stops along the way.

"And given that he was then a boy of eleven," Monsieur Chaput said, "with whom did he come? And for how long was he given permission to stay? These are crucial. If he entered the country and received permission for a stay of sufficient length, we can discover whether he is in Paris. And if he is, he should have an identity card and his domicile should be registered with the prefecture. It is all really quite simple."

My own experience in Berlin led me to believe that Monsieur Chaput was exaggerating. A teenage boy has a number of ways of eluding bureaucrats and busybodies. I'd watched them do it. But Monsieur Chaput clapped his hands together, settled with Jules the *petite question de l'argent*, that is to say his fee, and promised to have information one way or the other within a few days.

He was as good as his word. The next time Jules and I climbed up to his dusty office, Monsieur Chaput opened a folder and laid a series of document photographs on the desk. "Some good and some not so good news," he said. "Pavel Lagunov entered France at Marseilles on May 30, 1925. He was in the company of one Bogdan Anoshkin, nationality, Russian, age thirty-nine. The boy is listed as his nephew." He looked up at us quizzically.

"I will ask Inessa, but it is most unlikely. Their family was totally lost and scattered."

"The pair were granted entry for one year. Anoshkin lists his profession as banker." With a nod, he turned over another photograph. "In July of that year, Anoshkin secured an identity card for an address on the rue de l'Odéon. The address, *messieurs*, suggests he may indeed be a banker."

"And Pavel?"

"Now is the not-so-good news. Pavel is listed, yes. But when Monsieur Anoshkin moves in January 1926 to the rue de Fleurus, Pavel is not with him. Where is Pavel? And where is his new *carte d'identité d'étranger?* We do not know, *messieurs*." The detective's beaky nose twitched. This anomaly was deeply offensive to him.

"Monsieur Anoshkin lives on the rue de Fleurus, you say? He would be the man to talk to."

"Indeed," said Chaput, "but he left France in August 1926 for Turkey. Alone."

"But what does all this mean?" Jules asked anxiously.

"It could mean a number of things. Most sadly, it might mean the boy is dead. But"—here he held up his hand—"there is no record of his death. I have checked very thoroughly. He is not in the mortality records. Of course, there are those who die without an identity. Sadly, this is time consuming to check."

I exchanged glances with Jules. Our funds were strictly limited.

"There are other possibilities. He may have returned to Russia or left for some other country. There is no record of his departure from France, but people do cross borders unofficially."

"How likely is that for a boy of twelve or thirteen?" I asked.

"It is not very likely, but it does happen. Sometimes. There is also the possibility that he has changed his name, or had it changed for him. He might also be in custody. Some boys on their own commit petty crimes and come to the attention of the police. I will begin inquiries, but I think first, *messieurs*, you should find out if this Bogdan Anoshkin is a relative. If he is, there may be a way to contact him directly."

Jules nodded, thanked Monsieur Chaput, and shook his hand.

"It is good that we know he entered France and reached Paris," I said, for I could see how discouraged Jules was. "That is a start."

"Maybe a dead end, too."

"Berlin was full of boys on their own. Many had no documents, no identity cards, no permission from anyone for anything."

"Paris is not Berlin," Jules said.

We let the subject drop until we met Inessa at the theater. By arrangement, we had all arrived early, well before the rest of the cast and crew.

"You have talked to the detective," she said as soon as she saw us.

Jules nodded. "We have made progress, but only a little. Pavel got to Paris and was listed as living here, but after July 1925 he disappears from the residence records."

"I knew he was in Paris. I felt it. He is here. We will find him."

She went on about this until Jules put his hand on her arm. "Monsieur Chaput needs some more information," he said. "Pavel entered the country on May 30, 1925, supposedly with his uncle, a man by the name of Bogdan Anoshkin."

He started to ask if Anoshkin was a relative, but Inessa turned very white and began to wail in Russian. It was several minutes before Jules got her to sit down on the edge of the stage. She wiped her eyes, and in her now frozen features, I had an inkling of how she had survived; she converted great gusts of emotion to ice. "He is a bad man," she said. "A big party official. Corrupt, greedy, cruel."

"He lists his profession as banker," Jules said.

"He stole enough to start a bank. But what of that? He got fat while we were starving. There were many such. No!" She muttered in Russian for a moment, then, in French, "It was that he liked children. Young boys—and girls, too. A beast! How did he get his hands on Pavel?" She jumped up again. "I know how. And I know how I got to Paris and how Alexi got to Paris. You know how?"

Jules shook his head but I had a notion.

"Alexi sold Pavel for our exit visas and passage out of Odessa. 'He will be on the ship.' That's what he promised. 'It is not safe for us all to go together. Your brother will be there. It's all arranged.' I was fool enough to believe him. I would have died to save Pavel, but, right under my nose, he was sold to pay our passage!"

Jules tried to comfort her, but Inessa jerked away to stride back and forth. "I will kill him," she said, adding what sounded like imaginative Russian curses. "I will kill him."

Jules waited until she stopped, her hands clenched at her side, her lovely face distorted. "If you kill Alexi," he said quietly, "you'll wind up in jail with the guillotine in your future. What good would that do Pavel? How would that help him?"

"Don't give up yet," I said. "You were right all along. He got to Paris. Now he has disappeared, but probably he's still here!"

There was a long uncomfortable silence before Inessa would look at us, and then it was as if she saw us from a great height. "So! You are right. But I tell you now and you can believe it, if Pavel is dead, I will kill Alexi. Guillotine or no guillotine." Without another word, she went to her dressing room and closed the door behind her.

Jules sat down and put his head in his hands. "No need to worry about checking with the relief agencies," he said. "The boy is in the river. Or if he's alive, he's confined in some house. Dear God! At thirteen! Face of an angel. Worth, if Inessa is right, two visas and passage to Marseilles. Where else?"

Indeed, and that presented difficulties. If Jules was right, Pavel could have been outfitted with false papers, and fishing expeditions to find him wouldn't be easy as all the brothels kept in good with the police. I chose to imagine something else. "He might be on his own. Living hand to mouth around Pigalle."

Jules nodded. To his mind, that was hardly a happier prospect.

"Let us see what Chaput turns up. It's possible the police will know something about Bogdan Anoshkin and his French associates. While we're waiting, I will ask the street boys and search around the cafés, though it would be easier if we had a photo. A 'face like an angel' leaves a good deal to the imagination."

Jules shrugged. "It might not matter. A boy will have changed a lot in two years, especially if he has undergone hardships."

I'd seen something of what was possible along that line in Berlin, but there was no point in discussing that with Jules, who already had enough in the way of nightmares. Besides, if anyone knew who was young and Russian and trolling the cafés for trade of any type, it was my sometime pal Pyotr. QED as my old math teacher used to say. Pyotr had dangerous associates and serious troubles, but he was the man I needed to find. I figured that he owed me four pounds, five shillings' worth of help.

The difficulty was fitting a search into my busy schedule as the apprentice and Philip's lover. Even though Hector had replaced me on the machine, my evenings were still full, and Philip and I weren't moving in the right circles. Fortunately, I'm a creative liar, and I told Philip that my starchy and conventional ex-military uncle was in town. I worked this character up in my dad's image, gave him Uncle Lastings's tastes, and conjured plans for an evening at the Folies Bergère and visits to some of the less fancy cafés. "A real tourist evening in Paris," I told Philip, who agreed that it would be ghastly.

"But no more than your duty, my boy."

I picked up on his complacent tone. Had he cast his eyes elsewhere just before he was due to leave for home? Bad luck, Francis! I wanted Philip to land in London full of longing. I wanted to be summoned by telegram. I wanted an offer of help with the design studio that was growing sharper and clearer in my imagination without coming any closer to reality. What were my chances of a patron? Maybe not as good as I'd thought. Still, as Nan always reminds me, *There are other fish in the sea*, but maybe not too many would land in my net as well heeled and indulgent as Philip.

Nonetheless, I had promised Jules, and I believe in friendship. It tends to be more stable than romance. So I spent a frolicsome afternoon with Philip and ventured out on a circuit of the cafés and little restaurants that I knew Pyotr favored. No luck. A second supposed night with my "visiting uncle" brought no better results. The third night, I took off. It was Philip's last night in Paris, and we made it a good one. I remember large drinks, rich entrees, and sweet desserts, ending up at the Moulin Rouge with what Philip, slightly drunk by that time, called "our farewell to Barbette and all the joys of Paris."

After the performance, we went backstage, Philip shamelessly trading on my connection to the now mildly famous Les Mortes Immortels, and so capped the night with a visit to the famous aerialist's dressing room. Vander Clyde's English had a pronounced flat drawl that quite enchanted Philip. As usual, the trapeze artist had already removed his long blond wig and his elaborate ball gown at the end of his act, revealing, not a beautiful woman, but a compact, muscular man. The moment was such a surprising *coup de theatre* that I was almost reluctant to see him in ordinary clothes.

Philip, however, was insistent, so we squeezed in with the other well-wishers and fans to watch Barbette wipe off his makeup (amazingly subtle and good) and slither out of his trapeze tights and into a very handsome lounge suit. The goddess of the trapeze had vanished, and his metamorphosis complete, Monsieur Clyde thanked us for our compliments and strode off into the night.

"Amazing," said Philip in a wistful tone as we looked for a

taxi. "We are malleable creatures. The universe is ours and we don't know it."

I patted his shoulder, touched that even Philip, who I often found affected, had hidden longings, both suitable and unsuitable. That revelation moved me to ask, "Will I see you in London?"

His face closed up like a trap. "Oh, Francis! You belong to Paris, and I will never be able to think of you anywhere else."

As if, I thought, I was a sentimental rent boy with a poetic streak! I put him down right there as a coward and a hypocrite, and I did not see him off on the boat train the next morning, although he'd wanted me to go. But I decided *in vino veritas*: London was out, however sweet Philip was in the morning light of Paris. Instead, I finished up a rose-and-ivy design for Armand and took a little time at the easel to cut Inessa's head and neck from a poster I'd filched. I gave the image a masculine haircut before pasting it onto a clean sheet of paper. I toned down the full lips, erased the stage makeup with a grease pencil, strengthened the jawline, and darkened the eyebrows. Did the resulting image suggest a boy of thirteen with the face of an angel? We'd see.

I put the altered picture in my pocket, and by midday I had cast off caution and was headed back along the outer reaches of Vaugirard. Damn the Cossacks and full speed ahead! Or as Uncle Lasting would say, *Time to go over the top*. I was relying on two things: other distractions for Igor and his friends, and Pyotr's habits. To the best of my knowledge, my treacherous friend had only greeted the dawn once—the day he stole my four pounds, five shillings. Sluggish as Pyotr normally was even at noontime,

I thought that I had a good chance of catching up with him. Provided, of course, that he was still with us and not one of the unknowns floating in the Seine or unclaimed in the Paris morgue.

I wound up retracing the steps of my initial search for my light-fingered pal, but this time when I reached Trois Étoiles, the squat little café favored by Russian exiles, I was in luck. Early summer was kind to Trois Étoiles. The trees that overhung the roof cast a dappled shade on the outside tables, and tubs of pink geraniums flanking the doorway almost tipped the scruffy café toward the picturesque. But I wasn't thinking Impressionist scenes and Parisian charm, because sitting in a patch of shade with his big dark hat pulled low and both coffee and mineral water on the table in front of him—hangover remedies probably—was Pyotr.

CHAPTER EIGHT

"*Salut*," I said.

Pyotr's head snapped up, and his hand drifted south to the knife I knew he carried in his boot.

"*C'est Francis.*" I sat down uninvited. "You look as if you've had a hard night."

"The worst cognac imaginable. But you are angry?" Pyotr likes to have all the cards out on the table.

"I *was* angry," I said, emphasizing the past tense. "Perhaps you had good reasons."

"I did. I am sorry, Francis. I was sorry then, too, but I was running for my life."

I nodded. After meeting the Cossacks, I believed that. "But now you are sitting at an émigré café without a care in the world."

He shrugged. "I have cares aplenty, but Igor's no longer one of them."

"You have reached a rapprochement?" I was beginning to understand why French was long the language of diplomacy. It has so many nice shades of meaning, especially for selling out your friends.

"Igor is dead," he said flatly. "Order us a *vin blanc*, Francis, and we can toast the event."

At this welcome news, I signaled the waiter. The wine was poured, and Pyotr valiantly ignored his throbbing head to lift a glass.

"So what happened?"

"He made a mess with the business you know about. The commissars were unhappy to lose their man, and the mess made led them straight to Igor. What more to say?"

I thought that there was probably a lot to say. Like just whose faction was Igor in? And who had tipped off the faraway commissars? Not to mention who had actually dispatched the son of a bitch. Pyotr's face gave nothing away. But he was looking pretty spruce, hangover excepted. Those were handsome boots he was wearing, and although the hat was still big and black, it was definitely a fine new one. My four pounds, five shillings or a little payment for information rendered? *Mind your own business, Francis*, Nan said in my ear. She didn't have to add that any and all of Pyotr's Russian associates would be bad for my health.

"Fortunate for you," I said. "But you still owe me. Pounds sterling go a long way in Paris."

He raised his hands. "I'm a bit short at the moment."

"I'm not thinking of money. I need information. Perhaps you can give it to me."

His expression turned so cagey that I was sure this was not the first time Pyotr had been solicited for intelligence. "If I can, Francis. I am in your debt."

I reached into my pocket and took out my best guess at Pavel's features. "Would you have seen this boy?"

He glanced at the image and gave me a quizzical look. "This has been much altered."

"I do not have a photograph of Pavel Lagunov. That is an image of his sister. They are said to look much alike. The boy is thirteen, so think younger."

Pyotr examined the photograph carefully then shook his head. "I do not know him."

"Ever see anyone resembling him? Even in passing? I think he may be on the game."

"I see anyone like this, I would remember him. Russian, yes?"

"Yes, with a 'face like an angel,'" I said sadly. "His sister's description."

"Off on his own?" Pyotr's voice lost its habitual cool and cynical edge. I wondered how old he'd been when he decided to chance the streets.

"We believe so. He entered France roughly two years ago in the company of a man of very bad reputation. He'd been separated from his sister and her protector on the journey and was probably betrayed for money. Quite a lot of money, we think."

"A little money, the boy is dead," Pyotr said. "A lot of money? He's been sold."

"Where, Pyotr?"

"That I wouldn't know. Maybe out of Paris. There is always demand around ports." He looked at the photo again. "But this is a deluxe item. Only the best will do for the capital." There was a bitter edge in his voice. "We refugees are only so much raw material here, Francis."

"Where should I start to look?"

"You have a lot of money? Try the Hotel Marigny. Haunt of all the 'petite messieurs,' the gentlemen with money who buy whatever they want."

"Thirteen-year-old boys included?"

"If that's what the clientele demands."

"Anywhere cheaper?"

"There's a couple of other houses." He thought for a moment and mentioned some names. "Not so profitable. All the best people go to the Hotel Marigny—and invest in it, too."

"We will find a way to check. But will you keep an eye out for Pavel? Please. You can leave a message for me at the theater. Or—" I was about to give him my address but stopped. I liked Pyotr, but I didn't trust him. "Or with Jimmy at the Parnasse Bar."

"Certainly," he said. He emptied his wineglass and finished the mineral water, hints that he was about to be on his way and that I should be too.

"One other thing," I said, as I really hadn't yet gotten my pounds and shillings' worth. "Would you know anything about a man named Bogdan Anoshkin?"

The response was immediate. Pyotr straightened up, his face rigid. Then he recovered himself—Pyotr hadn't survived on the streets by accident—and shook his head.

"You don't know him? Supposedly a Soviet political official?"

Now he shrugged. "Maybe by reputation. I may have heard this or that."

"Even 'this or that' might be helpful," I said.

Pyotr sat silent.

"The boy is thirteen. He nearly starved to death after the revolution. He's lost everyone except his sister. If we can find him, he has a chance."

Now Pyotr stood up. "Stay away from Anoshkin. He is a dangerous man."

"Did he kill Igor?"

Now Pyotr smiled. "Anoshkin has another specialty altogether." He pushed back his chair and walked away.

A few hours later, I dropped the altered photo on Monsieur Chaput's desk. "His sister agrees it is a plausible likeness."

"This will be helpful," the detective said.

"Because of the boy's good looks, I asked around. The Hotel Marigny came up. Since Pavel hasn't been seen on the streets, that was my informant's best guess."

The detective made a dismissive gesture. "I will inquire," he said, "but the Hotel Marigny is a thoroughly respectable establishment. It is patronized by the sorts of people who do not wish to have any irregularities." Then he added, "Except the obvious," which, despite his dry tone and closed face, seemed by way of a joke.

I mentioned the other houses Pyotr suggested.

"A bit more likely," Chaput admitted. "But all these places are under the eye of the police. A boy, clearly underage, especially a boy confined against his will, this, *messieurs*, is unlikely."

Jules sighed. "However disagreeable the idea, we'd had hopes of finding him quickly. And the alternative . . ." His voice trailed off. I knew that he was wondering what he could tell Inessa.

"There are avenues yet," said Chaput. "Remember that there is no record of his death. And no unclaimed corpses of anywhere near the right age and description."

"Perhaps he was taken from Paris," I suggested.

Chaput surprised me by sharing Pyotr's opinion. He picked up the altered photo, looked at it again, and shook his head. "If the boy does look anything like his sister—oh, yes, I took in the show, dreadful except for the girl and the machines—he would be valuable to a certain clientele. My apologies, *messieurs,* to speak of him in these terms, but his beauty is his best chance for survival. With your permission, I will press on with our investigations."

He looked at both of us, and I looked at Jules. My personal exchequer would not stretch any further, but Jules nodded. "Time, Monsieur Chaput, is of the essence," he added and immediately rose to leave.

Out on the sidewalk, he seemed discouraged. "I'm afraid poor Pavel has eluded the record keepers. Although we must let Chaput proceed, I am not sure we have the right approach yet."

"I think Anoshkin is the key," I said. "He brought Pavel to Paris, purpose unknown since he apparently hasn't lived with the boy for over a year. That leaves us with Alexi. It would be good to know more about him. About his business here and whether he is still in contact with Anoshkin."

Jules shrugged. We both remembered Inessa's description of Alexi's changeable moods, late nights, and mysterious messages. "If Inessa cannot figure him out, who can?"

"Agreed," I said, but there was another possibility, one I did not yet feel able to mention to Jules. As soon as I finished my work for Monsieur Armand, an abstract pattern this time, much more to my taste than the everlasting bouquets—I swear, even in gouache, roses and lilies roused my asthma—I set off for my "French" uncle's antique shop.

Across the cobbled courtyard. Around to the converted stable. All quiet. I rang the bell. No answer. Was Claude out searching for antiques? Ormolu furniture, his specialty? If so, why was the little sign in the window not turned to *Fermé*? I tried the door. Locked tight. Had my uncle left in a hurry? Forgetful? That did not sound quite right. I looked around the silent courtyard; even the sounds of the street—a horse clopping by, the squeak of a cart, the hum of a motor—were muffled. No one in sight: no maid taking a break at the back of the town house; no chauffeur wiping down the Peugeot or the Citroën. There was no one to see me peering in the windows, at the front, then along both sides.

Possibly there was a rear entrance. I went quietly around to the back, where a small green van was parked near, yes, a back door. Unlocked, as it turned out. I stepped inside, caught a whiff of gas, and immediately began to wheeze in the toxic air: Call me the canary in the mine. "Claude!" I called, and when there was no answer, "Uncle Lastings!"

I pulled my shirt up over my mouth, propped the back door open, and hurried the length of the shop to unlatch the front door. I grabbed one of the cheap chairs to hold it open. Even with a through draft, the gas was almost overwhelming. I gasped outside for a moment, then stepped in again. Main showroom empty. Clutter of chairs and tables, likewise.

The workroom with its storage racks: I should have thought of that first—gas clearly affecting me. Down the corridor, lungs laboring like a steam engine, shove the workroom door, stuck. Locked? *Turn the handle, Francis!* Gas like a toxic cloud. "Claude! Claude!"

A faint moan. He was lying on the floor behind the big work-table. I grabbed one leg and staggered back, bumping him against the legs of the table and banging my shoulder into the painting rack before I reached the door. Hallway. *Better. It's better in the hallway,* I told myself, although I was unable to transmit that conviction to my lungs. They'd had enough. More than enough. I dropped Uncle Lastings's leg, and I think I'd have lunged for the back step and left him there if a sharp gust of wind hadn't blown through the corridor.

A gasp of clean air. I grabbed his arm and, stumbling, falling, crawling, reached the back door. Out! I dropped Uncle Lastings, head down and in the clean air, his legs still prone in the hallway, and fell to my knees in the yard. Lunch returned in a disgusting brown-and-yellow spatter. I wiped my mouth. My head was throbbing, and it took me several minutes in the open air to get to grips with the situation.

First thing, Francis, is to stand up. I stood. *Next thing is to remove Uncle Lastings from the doorway.* Done. *Loosen his collar, prop him up.* "Uncle Lastings! Claude!" His head lolled and there was no answer. *Help needed. Help beyond me.* I stood up, dizzy, the courtyard swaying and rippling and stumbled around the building to the main house. I hit the bell with the flat of my hand and kept it there, croaking, "*Au secours!*"

The door was opened by a starchy-looking maid, disapproval all over her face.

I could feel *mon français* drifting away in a cloud of carbons. "*Gaz! Gaz!*"

Right word. Gas is bad. Comes via mains. Threatens everyone.

"*Dans l'étable de mon oncle.*" Oops! *C'est la table de mon oncle*, beloved of French lessons. But no uncle. It was Claude. Correction: "*L'étable de Claude. Claude est tres malade!*" And I flapped my arm toward the back court, lost my balance, and wound up listing against the doorjamb and feeling a good deal removed from what became a frantic bustle. The maid rushed into the yard and began shouting for a doctor. Her mistress got on the phone, high speed and high volume, and a butler, tall and fat with a white moon face, extracted me from the door frame and maneuvered me into a chair.

From then on, it was safe for me to be a spectator. By the time the firemen arrived to see about the gas leak, and my uncle had been carried, I suspect by the maid and the butler, to a nearby doctor's office, I had recovered enough to speak intelligible French, to conceal my relationship with Claude, and to walk unassisted.

"You're very lucky," said the butler. "Enough gas to send the building into the clouds."

My lungs weren't impressed, and I wasn't either. Even in deep disguise as Claude, purveyor of ormolu, my uncle had managed to land me in the soup. Nonetheless, I nodded weakly and agreed that I'd been lucky. "And Monsieur Claude?" I tried for the right amount of concern. He was supposedly a casual acquaintance.

"Dr. Gallopin will see him right. He treated men gassed in the trenches. Monsieur Roleau couldn't do better anywhere in Paris."

"Perhaps I should visit him, too. I have lung trouble," I added and tapped my chest.

The butler agreed this would be prudent; he would escort me as soon as he had locked up the building. "Madame rents the building to Monsieur Roleau. She will not want any risk of his losing stock."

A few minutes later, he returned to report that the building was airing out nicely. The gas had been shut off, the corroded pipe would be repaired. Everything would be perfectly safe, he assured me, then took my arm and helped me down the block to the doctor's office. Claude was lying in the main consulting room with an oxygen mask over his face. The doctor took me into his office, listened to my lungs, and had me count backward to see if I was compos mentis.

My asthma was, he said, a complication. He would give me a little oxygen after Monsieur Roleau was finished with the apparatus.

"Will he be all right?" I asked.

The doctor was very tall and very straight backed with a mop of coarse black hair, a narrow face with high cheekbones and prominent eyebrows. He smelled of cigarettes and, faintly, of brandy. His manner was brisk; his speech, clipped. My uncle would find him sympathetic. He reminded me of my father and I found him less so.

"Should be. Oxygen is the best thing. You found him, I understand?"

"Yes. A friend of mine bought a quite valuable boule chest from him. I'd stopped by to check about the shipping and to see if he had acquired any similar pieces." Did that sound right? I'd clearly been mildly affected by the gas, too. I was finding it hard to tell if what I was saying was plausible, never mind true.

"Probably saved his life. Could you see him home afterward? He will be weak. You will be, too, but your exposure was not as severe."

"Certainly," I said, figuring that Uncle Lastings could at least come up with the doctor's fees and a cab.

When we left the office several hours later, my uncle still looked very peaked. The dyed red hair accentuated his pallor, and his large and vigorous body seemed to have come unstrung at every joint. He moved like an old man, although his mind seemed unaffected. He leaned heavily on my arm, and said, "Nice of you to see me home. It's Francis, isn't it? Philip's little friend? You saved my life, I'm told. Along with the good doctor here."

Gallopin was on the other side of him, and between us, we got my uncle into a cab. He leaned his head back and breathed heavily for several seconds. Dr. Gallopin waved, and when he returned to his office, Uncle Lastings asked the driver to take us first to the antique shop.

"You best not go in, Monsieur," I said *en français*. "There will still be gas."

He reached into his pocket for a ring of keys. "There's a Webley in the bottom drawer of the desk," he said in soft and rapid English, pointing to a small key. "Right side. And a box of papers. Authentications. Bring those to me. And lock the shutters." He took a big breath and collapsed against the seat again.

I gave him a look. I didn't fancy even one more molecule of gas. I fancied the Webley even less. The last time he'd had me fetch his service revolver, nothing good had happened.

"It was deliberate, of course," he added. "That building hasn't been lit by gas for twenty years. And I haven't had the heater on for more than a few hours in the last months."

"All right," I said. The cabbie pulled around to the back. I got out, unlocked the back door, and went through the building closing and locking the shutters, but leaving the windows partly open as there was still gas. In the front office, I unlocked the desk drawer and found the Webley wrapped in an old silk scarf. I stuck it in my belt. There was a small box of bullets. I put those in my pocket and closed the drawer. I was on my way out when I remembered that I was supposed to get a box of documents, not a box of bullets. Clearly, gas is bad stuff in more ways than one.

Back to the desk. I unlocked the drawer and found a reinforced green cardboard document box. Checked that it contained authentications, relocked the desk, and made my way out. In the cab, my uncle glanced at me. When I nodded, he gave the driver a nearby address that turned out to be a fine three-story building with a walled garden. Whatever Claude's tastes might be, my uncle prefers comfort, even luxury. I wondered who was paying the bills this time.

Out of the cab. He steadied himself on the car to pay the

driver, then draped his arm across my shoulders, staggering me with his weight. "Steady on," he said in English.

"I've had a bit of gas myself, you know."

"A mere whiff." Maybe he'd suffered more harm than I'd realized, because he started talking about gas attacks on the trenches. He stood on the sidewalk raving about clouds of chlorine, mustard, and phosgene gases and swearing like a trooper. I only got him into the house with difficulty, and I had to hand him the Webley before he would reveal his floor, the second, and his flat, directly across from the stair landing. I hoped he was not going to return to the western front like a dangerous chap I'd known in Berlin.

But the Webley had a calming effect and the box of bullets and the documents even more so. He unlocked the door to a big, square room with fine high windows. Shutters damped down the bright afternoon light; old but comfortable furniture and rose striped wallpaper completed the decor. My uncle—for despite the dyed hair and bad tailoring he was definitely Uncle Lastings once again—sat down heavily on the sofa. He examined the Webley with care and made sure it was loaded, before clicking on the safety and setting it on the table beside him. "We'll have a whiskey." He nodded toward a buffet well equipped with bottles and glasses. "Make mine a double."

I wondered if that had been part of the cure in the trenches.

I gave him a large glass and sat down across from him with a slightly smaller one, since my stomach had not fully recovered. "I need to know about Alexi," I said.

CHAPTER NINE

"Alexi tried to kill me," Uncle Lastings said heavily.

"Why would he do that?"

My uncle took another sip of whiskey. His color was returning as if the great northern cure-all was doing its work. "Greed, my boy. A serious vice, one of the Seven Deadly. You might not believe it, but I got part of my education from a curate."

I was afraid that my uncle's mind was becoming unfocused, maybe conveniently so. I cut off his reminiscences of the curate, a man devoted to foxhunting, pheasant shooting, and single malts, to ask, "Alexi. What is he? What does he do?"

Uncle Lastings studied the rose-patterned stripes as if seeking inspiration. "He does this and that," he said.

"Besides attempting to kill you with a leaking gas line."

My uncle sighed. "That's about the size of it."

"Not good enough." I was beginning to lose my temper. "What's he doing in France—besides whatever you two have going—and what's his relationship to a man named Bogdan Anoshkin?"

Well! Talk about the magic word. Uncle Lastings sat bolt upright. "What do you know about Anoshkin?"

Now the shoe was on the other foot. Now my uncle was desperately interested. Now I was the one considering the wallpaper and checking the technique on the roses: three tones of pink for the flowers, two of green for the leaves. I was thinking that they were not up to Armand's standard by any means, when my uncle, reviving by the minute, lunged over and seized the front of my shirt.

"Anoshkin!" he repeated.

I put my hand on his wrist. "I know something, but I have a friend in need. Maybe you can help."

He wasn't pleased at this appeal for mutual assistance, and I think he would have walloped the information out of me if he'd felt at all like himself. As it was, we went back and forth for a few minutes before he thought to ask why I was interested.

"Alexi has a hold over Inessa, and as she is part of the troupe of Les Mortes Immortels—"

He flapped his hand, dismissively. Not good enough.

"A friend of mine is in love with her."

"Romantic fool," said my uncle. "And more fool you to get involved."

Although I had to agree with him, I said, "You're lucky I did. If I hadn't come by today, you'd be in the Paris morgue. So what's Alexi's real business?"

He sighed and took another drink. "Alexi is ex-military, a political official whose real loyalties are uncertain. My best guess is that he's an assassin. The NKVD sends them out after dissidents, czarists, and old Bolshies who fall afoul of Comrade Stalin. Alexi fits the picture, and today confirms it. He's a professional."

Nothing that sinister had crossed my mind, but the idea did open possibilities. "He must have plenty to keep him busy in Paris," I said, thinking of the Cossacks and the murky political currents in the exiles' favored cafés. "Why bother with some scam with you?"

My uncle shook his head. Now it was my turn to contribute. "Anoshkin," he said and waited.

"He and Alexi were both political officials back in Irbit, where Inessa's family was in exile. The two Red officials knew each other there."

My uncle nodded in a knowledgeable way. "Inessa's people must have been minus six, exiles who had to live outside the big, strategic metropolitan areas."

"Irbit apparently qualified. Anyway, the parents died of TB and hardship, and Inessa came under Alexi's dubious protection. As you know already."

He nodded.

"What you maybe don't know is that Inessa really did have a brother, a younger brother named Pavel. When I told her that the boy had entered France with Anoshkin, she was horrified. Horrified that a man of his reputation had custody of her brother and horrified because she reckoned Alexi had sold Pavel to Anoshkin and used either his money or his influence or both to get her safely into France."

"How old was the boy? And what does he look like?" my uncle asked, all focused and less appalled than interested—I wasn't sure what that told me.

"He was eleven at the time with a face like an angel, according to Inessa. She stays with Alexi in the hopes of finding the boy in Paris."

"He could be anywhere."

"Ah, but he got to Paris." I gave him a digest of what Jules and I had learned from Monsieur Chaput. "Pavel and Anoshkin shared the same address until Anoshkin left for Istanbul a year ago. At that point, Pavel disappeared from the public records. What I need to know is who this Anoshkin is and what he's done with Pavel."

Uncle Lastings leaned back on the sofa without saying anything for several minutes. "Deep water, my boy," he said at last. "We're in deep water."

"But have we a chance of finding him?"

He thought a minute. "If he's alive and in Paris, probably. But it won't be easy. Anoshkin is, like his sometime friend Alexi, an NKVD specialist."

My uncle paused as if to gather scattered thoughts and raised his glass for a refill. I obliged. When I sat down again, he said, "Anoshkin's specialty is blackmail. His job is to collect damaging information about foreign diplomats, politicians, and military men, usually military attachés. Documents are good, but pictures are preferred." He gave me a questioning look to see if I understood.

"Must be tricky work."

"In Paris?" He gave a snort. "A bit harder than in Berlin but only just. Of course, your upscale brothel is not going to cooperate with a Soviet operative armed with a spy camera. Why would they? But Anoshkin could take another tack: He'll set up a honey-pot, a little private enterprise with someone very special."

"An underage boy of exceptional beauty."

"If that is the taste of the target, certainly. And I suspect it is. There are candidates in our embassy and probably in others," he said a trifle grimly. "Otherwise, it would have been less fuss all around to work with your friend Inessa."

"Unless Alexi insisted on keeping her for himself."

"Knowing Alexi, he would have sold either one or both. But who knows? Men are fathomless."

"I still don't understand why he ventured this painting scheme with you. Wouldn't it interfere with his other work?"

"Maybe he considered it a useful front," my uncle said, "or maybe he is tired and wants out. As no one gets to retire from the NKVD, I suspect Alexi's thinking of Argentina or the United States or Australia. Maybe with your friend's girl."

"He was not too tired to tamper with the pipe."

My uncle shrugged eloquently and ran his hands through his dreadful red hair. Perhaps he was returning to Claude after all. "Old habits die hard, and he's greedy. Plus," he added after a moment, "he doesn't trust me."

If he expected me to be shocked at this, he was due to be disappointed. "He planned to kill or disable you and remove the paintings?"

"I think that's likely. I thought I had a bit more time to let the Matisse dry. But I was weak on the perimeter, my boy, a fatal error every time. I was forgetting that Alexi knows nothing about art. Unlike me, who's had a good advisor." He leaned over and patted my knee. "As for the paintings, I suspect he's there now."

I couldn't help glancing at the Webley.

"Don't think of it. A shoot-out in that quartier would jeopardize other plans. And Alexi will be an excellent shot and hard to surprise."

He sounded so sensible that I thought the gas had caused real damage until he winked. "Best of them already in transit," he said. "I didn't trust him, either."

He laughed and raised his glass, but I was uneasy. In the course of a fraud, admittedly an amusing one, my uncle had managed to offend a professional assassin, who'd already nearly killed him. Here we sat, hungover with gas, in a flat that would be all too easy for a man of Alexi's skills to locate. Was Uncle Lastings a good shot? I very much hoped so.

"Not to worry," my uncle said. "He wouldn't know a Rembrandt from a postcard artist."

"Though he will surely have counted the paintings."

"Perhaps he has his reasons for leaving prematurely," Uncle Lastings said. "I believe that your ridiculous theatrical is winding down?"

"Last show tonight," I said.

"It's the perfect time to leave with the paintings and the girl. Too bad for your friend."

I got up at this.

"Where are you going?"

"If you're right, we have to get Inessa away from Alexi, for now she will leave him. When she learns what Anoshkin's about, I know she will."

"You will upset everything." My uncle picked up the Webley.

I found that, like Pyotr, I preferred to have all the cards on the table. "Would you shoot me, Uncle Lastings?"

"I'm full of family feeling, my boy, but Claude might."

I sat down again on the edge of the chair. "Will Alexi take the van?"

"He does not have the keys. He will have had to make other arrangements."

"So we get the van, and my friend and Inessa leave from the theater before Alexi shows up as usual with the cab. What would that cost you?"

"Quite a lot if he spots the van. He couldn't help but recognize it. And disaster if we should meet him at the shop."

Uncle Lastings did not sound eager, but I picked up on the pronoun, *we*. "You always say, 'Get the civilians out of the firing line.' Get Inessa and my friend away, you've got a clear field of fire." Was that the right term? I had the feeling I was mixing my military metaphors. Maybe the gas had affected me, too. "Besides, if Inessa isn't being watched every minute, she can help in the search for Pavel."

My uncle sat toying with the Webley as if we had all evening when, in fact, it was only two hours till curtain time, and I still had to convince Inessa and devise a plan with Jules. That was assuming Alexi delayed their departure until after the show. Would he do that or would he say the hell with the Theatrical Imperative—the show must go on? I needed to leave; at the same time, I sensed negotiations had reached a delicate point.

Uncle Lastings is never without what he calls an exit strategy.

He is also rarely without irons in the fire: note the plural. *Patience, Francis*, Nan said in my ear, and I made myself lean back in the chair, although I couldn't help jiggling one foot.

My uncle noticed and smiled, showing his bad dentistry and long canines. I had not noticed before how doggy his mouth looked. There was a pause before he said, "I think we should let bygones be bygones, in the interest of presenting a united front."

Shades of his last scam involving pamphlets that advocated, if I remembered right, a *United Front Against Barbarism and Communism*. A fat lot of good that idea had done.

"I might be able to put some help your way," he continued.

"When? The play closes tonight. The only time Inessa is out of Alexi's sight is when she's on the boards. Or posing for your pictures. Tonight's our last chance—unless he leaves before the show. He might, you know. He might pack the goods and try to force Inessa to go before the performance. Do you know where they stay? Jules probably knows." I jumped up in agitation, and my uncle again told me to sit down.

"Coolness under fire is essential," he said.

"You don't understand. If we can't get her away, she'll kill him. Or try to. She'll never forgive him for Pavel. Never. And I doubt she will be able to hide her feelings much longer."

"Timing is everything in war and love," my uncle agreed, then added, "I can supply a vehicle." He waved his hand. "I will call my landlady's butler."

"If Alexi is at the shop . . ." I began. The butler had been kind. I didn't think that throwing him in the way of an NKVD assassin was a good idea.

Uncle Lastings was unperturbed. "Luc is a resourceful chap who has a key to the van. Your part will be to get Inessa and your friend out of the theater well ahead of the final curtain. I can collect them."

I saw a dozen little problems with this, but it could work. It was possible—if I could leave this very minute, preferably with money for a cab. I needed to talk to Jules and Inessa. There were arrangements to be made for the machines and for a stand-in for Human Hope, a mass of details that made my head, already aching from the gas, throb some more.

My uncle nodded sagely. "It can be done by a boy of your abilities. In the interests of time, I will say no more. But I need something in return."

I was already halfway to the door. "Yes," I said, eager to be gone. "I'll give you a hand."

"That's the spirit that built the empire," my uncle said.

Which really should have warned me, but I was thinking of the performance and of what could be adjusted and of everything that could possibly go wrong.

Uncle Lastings gave me some francs for the cab. "Curtain comes down at what—nine? Nine thirty?" he asked.

"Never later than nine twenty."

"Nine then. Twenty-one hundred on the nose. Stage door."

"Right."

"Come by tomorrow, and I'll brief you on our next step."

I agreed, of course; what else could I do? Then I hustled down the stairs and out to the street. I found a taxi on the boulevard and stopped first at the apartment to pick up Jules. On the way to the theater, I gave him an account.

"But can we trust this Claude Roleau? You said yourself he's a scoundrel."

I'd expected resistance from Inessa but not from Jules.

"Of course he's a scoundrel. I know; he's my uncle. But I saved his life today and that's put him in a helpful mood. That and the gas."

"Your uncle!"

More explanations necessary. We arrived at the theater with Jules only half committed and no plans for anything. Fortunately, Inessa, better acquainted with the NKVD, heard me out with clenched fists. "I will kill him. I will kill them both."

"But not yet, Inessa. There is a chance to find your brother. If Claude is correct, there is a chance, and it won't be just us looking for him, either. So you have to go tonight."

Her face was set.

"You'll need to leave the stage nine sharp. Out the stage door with Jules. There will be a green works van. Get straight into it and go. Jules will think of somewhere. Or Claude will have an idea."

She thought no, and then she thought yes. You can bet there was a discussion about this, ending with the conviction that it could be managed. Maybe.

"You can take my machine," Jules said. "For the last few minutes."

"Human Hope disappears," Inessa said. "That is a problem."

"Leandres will be furious," Jules said, "but the audience won't know the script."

"It's hard to follow in any case," I said.

"When there is no Human Hope at the final curtain—"

"You will already be gone."

"And then we start the search for Pavel," she said. "Then we start in earnest."

CHAPTER TEN

Jules gave me a hasty lesson on his machine. I was to work a lever that swung the steam shovel–like head around, not very taxing except the motions had to be coordinated with both lights and music. I struggled to tell one tune from another and found this assignment so tricky that we decided I would only take over at the last minute. Inessa packed her street clothes in a borrowed sack, and everything was ready for her quick departure with Jules until the houselights gave their preliminary dimming. It was Inessa's habit to check the house at this point. We could already tell from the rustling of programs and the clatter of seats out front that it would be a good finale, and the atmosphere backstage was buoyant.

I was standing in the wings when she drew her head back from the gap in the curtain, her face stricken.

I touched her shoulder. "What is it?" I whispered.

"Alexi is in the house! Front row center. He is waiting to see the show!" Inessa began muttering in Russian. "He suspects something. I know he does."

A major complication, making everything more delicate and dangerous—or did it? "He can't be waiting in the alley if he's sitting in the theater," I said, thinking that Uncle Lastings would be safe in the van whenever he came.

"He'll see me disappear!"

"You vanish backstage several times. He won't know the stage business has been changed. He'll expect your return right until the curtain calls."

Inessa shook her head. "But Jeanne's dialogue makes no sense without Human Hope. Everyone will know something is amiss. And Alexi, you know, he sleeps with one eye open."

In my opinion, Mademoiselle Berger's dialogue made little sense even under the best circumstances. "We'll think of something," I said quickly. "Remember, just at nine, Jules gives you the signal, that little extra blast from his machine's horn. It's your best chance to leave. And to find Pavel. Remember that."

She bit her lip, gave me a hug, and nodded.

"Places, everyone!" Monsieur Leandres called.

Houselights down all the way. A soft shuffling as the performers found their marks. Music, courtesy of our violin, clarinet, drum, and piano, rose from the pit for the last Parisian performance ever of Monsieur Leandres's great Surrealist Entertainment. I made my way from the wings to the machines. "Alexi's in the house," I whispered to Jules.

Jules began to swear under his breath. "Is he armed? Does he carry a weapon?"

Something I'd not considered. "I don't know. Inessa spotted him out front."

"Christ! That's all we need. What a nightmare."

"But if he's in the house, you'll have a clear exit from the stage door."

"The play falls apart without Human Hope. It will be obvious Inessa's gone. And what he might do then is anyone's guess."

"Someone's got to take her place. What about Duguay?"

"He has shoulders like a rugby fullback. And he has to lift Human Hope at the end."

Oh, right. Another of Leandres's symbolic touches. "What about LePage?" As soon as I mentioned him, I realized that he was no good, either. He was much taller than Duguay, and he'd have no time to get out of his own complicated costume and into something approaching Inessa's white gown.

Jules shook his head. "Terrien's out, too. He's got to work the rigging for the flies."

"Well, there's Mademoiselle Berger's niece." She hadn't been a great success, but she was slight and female. "Where does she work?"

"Over by the Opera. She'd never arrive in time." Jules wiped the sweat from his face. Out of the corner of my eye, I saw Leandres giving me a glare. His performers were supposed to be focused all the time.

Not possible for me, but I do find there's nothing like a crisis to help in the concentration department. "Wigs, Jules. Are there wigs?"

"Maybe. They'd be downstairs in the costume store."

I edged back from the machine, waited until one of the so-popular shadows filled the background, and made my return to the wings. Ignoring a hissed question from Leandres, I clattered down the metal stair to the hallway and the storerooms beneath the stage. Props and bits of scenery leaned against the walls, along with cleaning supplies, extra rope, light fixtures, and lengths of wood. Two doors down was the costume store, crammed with racks of frocks and jackets and men's trousers in all lengths and styles. There were capes, hats, and gowns, many of them tiny, not too many of them white. I considered a satin number, a touch risqué for Human Hope, but marvelously suitable for Inessa, before I spotted a toga in the men's section. It would have to do despite an ugly purple border with a gold link design.

Wigs, now. Much less choice. A couple of powdered deals left over from a costume drama. A frightful black thing suitable for Medea, and several old man–old woman affairs that suggested a Human Hope on her last legs. I folded the toga over my arm and went upstairs. Dim sounds of laughter and applause. By some quirk in popular taste the Surrealist Entertainment had become a favorite with the arty crowd.

As I reached the corridor to the dressing rooms, Mademoiselle Berger came hustling out of the wings; the Voice of the Earth only appeared intermittently in the action.

"Francis! Come to bid farewell to our little production? And perhaps collect a souvenir?" She nodded toward the toga with a sharp, suspicious glance.

I decided to trust to her goodwill. "We need help, Mademoiselle. Inessa is running away with Jules."

"Ah," said Mademoiselle. "An elopement! Good for her! I always thought that surly Russian was no good."

"No good at all, but he's in the center row tonight. And he might be armed."

Mademoiselle rolled her eyes. "This is an excess of drama, Francis. Very romantic, very exciting, but more melodrama than surrealism."

"To avoid Alexi, they are leaving at nine on the dot. We'll have to fake the rest, Mademoiselle. For Jules's machine, maybe Duguay would take the last few minutes?"

"To assist Mademoiselle Inessa? Of course, that goes without saying. I will tell him. I am, after all, the Voice of the Earth."

"Thank you. That would be excellent," I said. I was sometimes unsure just when Mademoiselle was joking.

"Human Hope is quite another matter." Mademoiselle made a face.

"She has no lines. Whoever takes her place just stands."

"Providing a vision of ethereal beauty," Mademoiselle said drily. "I think the lights must be very low from nine on. Get into the wings and inform Terrien. He will pass the word to the rest and to the lighting technician. Everyone must know, every member of the cast. We must all be on high alert." Having expressed a sensible disapproval, Mademoiselle Berger now seemed enthusiastic, even excited.

"Yes, of course, and, Mademoiselle, it would be good to find a blond wig."

She gave me a look and held out her hand for the toga. "I have fifteen minutes more or less. Come straight back to my dressing room, and we will see what we can do."

I had not taken Leandres's references to our "theatrical family" seriously, but now it seemed I had only to mention Inessa, universally admired, and Jules, universally liked, to see the group close ranks. The lights would be dim. The ushers alerted. Old Jacques, the doorman, would keep watch for my uncle's arrival and alert for any sign of Russian reinforcements.

Back in Mademoiselle Berger's dressing room, I found her combing out a blond wig. It had a towering topknot and long side curls with a sort of horse's tail in the back.

"Grecian," she said as I came in the door. "Suitable for a Muse of Poetry, I believe. Or maybe Messalina. It could pass for Roman and it really looks more her style. Try it on."

The wig was a scratchy number that tickled the back of my neck and provoked a laugh from Mademoiselle Berger. "Ah, Francis, you are a real trouper." She turned me so that I could look in the mirror. Anyone less like Inessa would be hard to find. This was a crazy idea even if it was my own.

"The houselights better be all the way down," I said.

"Nothing a few inches of makeup can't cure. Do what you can with the toga, and when I come back, I'll do your face."

I must have looked doubtful because she added, "You must go on to save Inessa. And she will be good, I think, for your melancholy friend."

I nodded. I was for it; our theatrical family expected no less. I spent the next twenty minutes struggling with the toga. I rolled up my shirt and wrapped it twice around my chest and tied the sleeves to make a band. I took off my socks and stuffed them strategically into the shirt. I left my trousers on, thinking I might have to make a quick exit, but I rolled up the legs so that my bare feet would show properly. Why on earth muses and spirits of this and that have to be barefoot is beyond me. My personal muse, if I ever acquire one, will have fishnet stockings and quality footwear.

At five minutes to nine, Mademoiselle Berger breezed in. I'd done what I could with the toga, and I'd been dabbling with her makeup, whitening my face, darkening my eyebrows, and lining my eyes. Her professional assessment was, "not bad." She took up a brush and tried to give my round face cheekbones. This was only moderately successful. She took another, smaller brush and put shadows over my eyes. By this time it was two minutes to nine. I could almost hear Jules's warning toot.

"I'd better get to the wings," I said, but Mademoiselle Berger was a pro, and there was a spot of paint to be applied here and a tuck to be put in the toga there. She didn't let up until we heard the signal from Jules's machine. I jumped up from the chair, hustled out the door, and almost collided with Inessa hurrying from the stage with Jules right behind her, carrying her sack.

"*Bonne chance!*" I said and Inessa turned, looking flushed and lovely even with her eyes dark and enlarged with fear.

"*Merci*, Francis!"

Jules gave a wave as they bounded down the steps to Jacques's booth and the stage door.

In the wings, I strained my eyes for Inessa's green chalk marks. As if it would matter! But some of the cult of the theater must have rubbed off on me, because I not only spotted the marks but began rehearsing Inessa's last appearance. What was required? Solemn walk from the rear corner of the set. Forward to the marks, which must be found without looking down. Arms raised—I could manage that, they're my best feature—with an *expression of transcendent hope and joy* to quote Leandres. That was probably not on.

Music rising, cast milling about—I believe this represented Human Confusion but opinions differed. Hector all smooth and practiced on my old machine. Duguay was not so sound on the other for the head was weaving about in an alarming manner though the shadows were certainly dramatic. And out in the house?

Dazzled by the stage lights, I saw the theater as a black void. Was Alexi still there? And what was he doing? I hoped he was not even now lining up for a shot at his faithless love. *Don't think of it, Francis!* But the idea made its way from brain to legs to feet, which refused to move until Leandres stepped behind me, and with a great shove and the command, "*Marks!*," sent me across the stage just as the final drumroll—the Storms of Human Life—began.

I stumbled, stubbed one bare toe, hopped, caught myself, and commenced what I thought was a slow and solemn walk but obviously was a bit faster than that, as LePage hissed, "*Slower, slower*," from behind his outsize mask, and there was a little ripple of laughter and unease somewhere out in the darkness beyond the footlights. So, slow! Slower! I risked a glance down. A green scuff on the boards. Look up. Violin beginning in the pit, a thin wail that better ears assured me was quite lovely. Raise arms and think, not of the impossible *transcendent hope and joy* but of the safe escape of Jules and Inessa.

Actors who had been sprawled on the floor now arose and began stepping forward, the piano joining in with the violin and the thought crossed my mind that we were actually going to pull this off when suddenly the spotlight came up. Human Hope was bathed in white light and there was a shout: "*Inessa!*"

I lowered my arms. A seat clattered as a figure lunged toward the stage, igniting an uproar in the theater such as the Surrealist Entertainment hadn't seen since its opening nights. I started backing away from the footlights. The other actors jumped up, and Mademoiselle Berger shouted for the curtain. A rumble above and the heavy velvet drapes began their descent. I whipped off the blond wig and shrugged off the toga. The curtain began to bulge and sway as Alexi, it had to be Alexi, crossed the footlights and thrashed against the fabric looking for an opening.

At this, Duguay and LePage rushed to push back against the curtain, which bulged and billowed like a giant amoeba. Beyond, the auditorium was in an uproar, and Leandres stepped out at the extreme side of the stage in an attempt to calm the crowd. We could hear him shouting, "*Messieurs, Mesdames!*," and imploring everyone to be tranquil.

All he did was to indicate an entrance for Alexi, who leaped back, causing Duguay and LePage to tumble forward over the footlights and into the house, while the Russian charged our director. Leandres wound up flat on his back, and Alexi more or less fell onstage after him. With my exit through the wings blocked, I dropped behind my old machine and slipped inside the compartment.

Alexi kept shouting for Inessa, although Monsieur Leandres,

who had gotten back on his feet, was attempting to assure him that Inessa was no longer in the theater and that he, Leandres, personally knew nothing of her whereabouts. Rather than calm Alexi, all this did was to turn his attention to "*le garçon*" who had impersonated her. You can bet I kept my head down, but I might well have been discovered if Messieurs LePage and Duguay had not picked themselves off the floor and, reinforced by some of the sportier types in the audience, attacked the stage.

I looked out cautiously from the shadows around the machines. The actors and several audience members were attempting to subdue Alexi, who seemed more than their match. Their numbers began to tell, however, and it looked as if he was going to be brought down on the floor when there was a terrific bang and a ricochet off something metallic high up in the fly loft.

Instantly, cast and recruits dived toward the curtain, the machines, or the scenery, and Alexi charged through the wings toward the dressing rooms. I stuck my head out of the machine. Leandres was alone on his hands and knees, and my first thought was that he'd been shot. I clambered out, touched his shoulders and his back. "Are you hurt? Have you been hit?"

"No, no," he said, struggling to his feet. "This is an outrage! Riots, yes. Catcalls, yes. Rotten fruit, yes. But shots? Never in the history of the theater! The police will be informed." He was threatening to contact the Soviet embassy when he took an unsteady step forward, and I had to keep him from toppling. As we stood swaying together on the stage, Mademoiselle Berger's contralto rang out from the dressing rooms. Alexi had a pungent vocabulary, but Mademoiselle's was not far behind. Her voice gave the rest courage, and the actors, our director, and a good half dozen of the audience surged through the wings to the corridor.

We heard one last shout of "Inessa!" before a clatter on the stairs. A warning from old Jacques, then the stage door slammed. Alexi was gone, and although there were congratulations and boastful remarks all around, no one seemed keen to follow him. I had dropped the toga in my haste to hide in the machine and now struggled to unwind my shirt. In Mademoiselle Berger's dressing room, I found my discarded shoes. I took a towel and wiped my face. She had not been joking about the inches of makeup.

The rest of the cast and our citizen volunteers soon appeared, including Terrien, down from his perch up on the catwalk. Leandres, who had sustained a cut lip and what looked to be a black eye, poured drinks for everyone from a very welcome bottle of cognac. Mademoiselle Berger arrived, assisting Jacques, who'd been knocked off his high stool beside the stage door. "Like a flash, gentlemen! Like a whirlwind, Mademoiselle! Out the door before I could stop him. I said, 'No one but the cast uses that door,' but he was like a bull with the red flag."

"No one blames you," Mademoiselle said kindly. "There was carnage on the stage! But no one seriously hurt, I don't think."

"No, no," said Leandres, "thanks to our valiant troupe and to friends of the theater." He made a big sweeping bow toward the recruits from the audience, who seemed willing to overlook the many deficiencies of the performance and the absence of a creditable Human Hope in exchange for budget cognac and the excitement of the evening.

"Though there was a shot," said Duguay. "Someone might have been hurt, even killed."

This idea was, as Nan would say, like a sweetie in their mouths. Everyone had an idea or an observation, and I think the total number of shots had reached five and would have gone higher if Leandres had not mentioned the police. I realized that he had not yet called them. This was a hopeful thought.

"Alexi will be long gone," I said.

But, protested the group, a dangerous man was on the loose, the public must be protected, such an outrage could not go unreported.

"Yes, yes," said Mademoiselle Berger. "That is all true in theory, but we must think of Inessa and Jules, to whom we owe so much. To bring this incident to public notice will maybe endanger them."

"Meanwhile, that crazy Russian is on the loose," said Terrien.

"He threatened Francis, didn't he? Didn't I hear that?" LePage asked.

Press coverage, questions from the police! Did I want that when I had just committed myself to one of Uncle Lastings's schemes? No, indeed. "I didn't take that threat seriously," I said.

"Though he was promising you a slow and painful end," LePage added.

"With the police comes press coverage just before our provincial venture," said Leandres. "That might be extremely valuable."

"Questions from the police might also delay your departure," I suggested.

"Oh, no, all is scheduled," said Leandres, but his face fell.

He'd been kidding himself that he could have the publicity benefits of the latest ruckus without any of the inconveniences.

"And for myself, questions and publicity—well, wouldn't they attract Alexi's attention? I don't know where Jules and Inessa have gone, but he will be convinced that I do, and as Jules's friend, I'm a target for sure."

"Francis is right," said Mademoiselle Berger, whose vast theatrical experience gave her opinions extra weight. "And I think that you must not go home tonight, Francis, in case Alexi knows where you live. It is possible that he does."

There was general agreement about this because Jules and I had rooms in the same building, and Inessa might have let the address slip. The cast had a solution. Duguay and Terrien were to strike the set along with LePage, who would drive the truck. They assured me that I would be welcome to stay and help. "We plan to sleep in the truck. No one think of you there," LePage said.

"And as you helped build the machines, you will know something about how to disassemble them," Duguay added.

I could foresee a lot of work and an uncomfortable bed, but I said, "Right. Thanks."

Leandres clapped me on the shoulder. "Members of Les Mortes Immortels stick together," he said. "And we are not without friends." This with a bow to the audience members who had come to our defense. The cognac bottle went around again, and Mademoiselle Berger, clearly a woman of infinite resource, produced not one, but two, bottles of wine as well as a box of biscuits.

There was a good deal of merriment before the stage crew and

I got onto the set, and a good deal of work before we all climbed into the loaded truck. LePage drove us several blocks to a court-yard closed with high, metal-reinforced gates. When he shut off the engine, Duguay jumped out to close and latch the gates. He and LePage bedded down in the front seat, leaving Terrien and me to settle as comfortably as we could amid the blankets and tarps that protected the disassembled machines and the various flats and props. The sky was beginning to lighten before I fell asleep to dream of houses that looked a lot like the stage of our theater and of running men pursued by shots.

CHAPTER ELEVEN

The creak of a bicycle, the rattle of a metal door or gate opening, street noises. I sat up, knocked my head on the truncated arm of one of the machines, swore, and woke up completely. I wasn't in my comfortable Left Bank room, a dwelling I suspected was gone forever. Paris seemed a city for night flits, and I hoped I'd be able to recover my clothes, my extra pair of shoes, and my books. Just where was I now? Someone was snoring behind a stylized tree last seen on the stage with Les Mortes Immortels. I was with the set and machines in a truck that smelled strongly of sweaty bodies and gasoline. I'd lain down sometime in the wee hours and now.

I listened. One of the city's bells was tolling the hour, a great many strokes. Could it possibly be ten A.M.? Yes, it could and the apprentice was monumentally late. I stumbled out of the truck, stuck my feet in my shoes, and opened the small door set into the courtyard gate. I walked until I found a street sign and made my way to the Metro. I got to Armand's just after eleven.

"You must have had a hard night," was his comment.

I ran my hand over my face and saw a smear of greasepaint. "I was pressed into service at the theater," I said, "for a lady in distress."

"*Quelle surprise!*" Armand was in a bad mood.

"Also a closing-night fracas, striking the set, and a lot of very bad cognac." The latter was probably behind the headache that reached from the back of my skull to just over one eye.

I sat down at the worktable and reached for one of the fine Canson sheets to begin.

"Don't touch the paper! Your hands are filthy!"

I got up and started toward his bathroom to wash, but this didn't suit Armand, either. The apprentice was late, unconscionably late, and had arrived in no condition to work. I gave him a look. I knew perfectly well that a full account of the evening's events, emphasizing the more amusing and scandalous aspects, would put him right. Give Armand a tidbit on the latest outrage or a bit of gossip fresh from the street, and he was a happy man. But I didn't feel like it. I was sick of being bullied and of doing a great whack of work for only a whiff of profit. I'd seen what he charged for the rug I designed, and I'd about given up hope of a fair deal from him.

"Fine," I said. "Settle up with me for this week's work and I'm off."

He didn't want to pay me, pretended he had no money on hand, and thought it best I come back "early next week."

I sat back down at the desk and folded my arms. I suspected that he had a client coming—or someone else of interest—because after a few minutes of huffing and puffing, he produced a handful of francs. He'd shorted me but not too badly, and while he was fetching the money, I'd helped myself to several good drawing pencils and a new eraser. I figured we were even.

The bells were ringing for quarter to twelve when I left, and I didn't get farther than out the door and around the corner before a horn tooted and the green antiques shop van pulled up beside me. Uncle Lastings looked all bright and bushy-tailed, in contrast to me. I'd caught my reflection in Armand's hall mirror, pale, paint smeared, filthy, and exhausted. I'd been in no mood for Armand, and I was in no mood for my uncle, either. If I hadn't been anxious to learn about Jules and Inessa, I'd have ignored him and walked on.

"Get in," said my uncle.

I opened the door. "Are Jules and Inessa safe?"

My uncle does a very good impression of astonished incomprehension. "Safe? Of course, they're safe. Tickety-boo. I collected them myself, twenty-one hundred hours on the dot. Drove at legal speed to deposit them in the safe house, a late supper included."

I was relieved to hear that and said so.

"You underestimate me, my boy. But mum's the word on their location. Best you know nothing. What one doesn't know, one can't tell."

So true—if melodramatic.

"You're very quiet," said my uncle after a few more minutes. He drove with considerable élan—another side of him, chauffeur extraordinaire.

"I've lost my job with Monsieur Armand, and I've probably lost my room and all my possessions."

"Oh," said my uncle airily, "mere things of this world."

"As I recall, you're rather fond of them yourself."

"But always ready for the call of king and country." He glanced at me. "Fortunately for you, because I have maintained my contacts with certain branches of our government and with old comrades from the war, you now have other employment. As for clothes." Another look. "We can sort those. You'll see. Probably nothing you had was suitable, anyway."

I looked out the window. We seemed to be heading west toward the Bois de Boulogne. I saw the mass of greenery and felt my nose twitch. Pollen is my enemy. That decided it. "If I'm going to work, I'll need to be paid."

"All expenses, of course," my uncle said. "His Majesty's government is fair if not lavish. Must think of the rate payers, you know."

The last time I'd assisted His Majesty's government, I'd wound up in torturous heels impersonating a hatcheck girl, and all I'd gotten out of it was a second-class ticket to Paris. "Not good enough," I said. "I need fifty pounds."

"Fifty pounds!" My uncle sounded as shocked as if I'd asked for the *Mona Lisa* and a concession at the Eiffel Tower. "Your indulgent mother sends you five a month and you live on that quite nicely. What on earth would you do with fifty pounds?"

"I'd think of something," I said. "But whatever it is, I'm not working for less. Half in advance."

Uncle Lastings took this seriously enough to pull over to the curb and park. "Now, see here. I kept my part of the bargain and got the lovebirds to safety. Glad to do it. Your friend is an officer and a gentleman. Now you keep to your word."

"Certainly," I said, "but last time, I wound up not just leaving the city but leaving the country. Next step is back across the Channel, and I want money for Nan."

"Your nanny?" Considering how rackety and unconventional his own life was, I felt his surprise unwarranted.

"We're taking a flat together in London. With twenty-five pounds in hand, she can leave her present situation and find us rooms. Another twenty-five will enable me to join her and start work as a designer. If that's too much, you can jolly well find someone else."

My uncle appealed to my patriotism, to my affection for Jules, to the need to find Pavel quickly. On a normal day, I might have given in, but tired, hungover, out of work, out of clothes, and out of patience, I held out. Later that morning, we dispatched a postal order for twenty-five pounds to Nan. As so often with my uncle, our positions were now reversed: I was jubilant, as jubilant as I was going to be with a hangover and little sleep. He was grumpy—I suspect the twenty-five pounds came out of his own exchequer and reduced the profit from his fiddle with the paintings.

Out near the Bois, he pulled into the gated drive of a handsome building that he announced would be our base of operations and parked the van in the garage. He unlocked the ground-floor apartment and told me to get cleaned up and rested. "We begin tonight," he said.

I bathed and had a sandwich, but before I took a nap—important you look your best, my uncle insisted—I took some time at the handsome desk to write Nan.

I have sent you twenty-five pounds to find us rooms in London. Do that as soon as possible. Nothing fancy needed but something that will suit you and with a room I can use for a design studio. I know this is a surprise, but He Who Must Not Be Named has secured a job for me, and this time, I have asked to be paid half in advance. You can see I am getting wise to the ways of the world.

In the meantime, I am nicely situated in a fine room near the Bois de Boulogne. I will get a postcard for you soonest. It is where the gentry ride and go to the races; also there are gardens. He Who Must Not be Named is English again, which is a relief, and he has dyed his hair back and gotten proper clothes, which are also improvements. Exactly what I am to do is uncertain, but it requires fine new clothes and the special talents of your Francis.

More than that I could not tell her because my uncle waited until after our supper at a local café. I was interested to see that he was known by the proprietor, suggesting that while he had been living as Claude in one quartier, he had been Lastings in another. My uncle is a complicated man. As we drank our coffee, I was aware of him studying me. Well, let him look. I was dressed in a fine new shirt—real silk—with a lightweight summer suit, a linen between brown and gray. Whoever had picked it out had excellent taste. I had new, only slightly uncomfortable, shoes, and my hair had been lightened up by a gent who'd arrived late afternoon with a full hairdresser's kit. In short, I was done up like a prize pup, and if I'd ever looked better, I don't know when.

"Too bad you're not younger, Francis," he said at last.

"Berlin aged me."

My uncle sniffed and decided not to discuss Berlin. "Still you might do, Francis. Though a couple of years younger would be desirable, I have confidence in your abilities."

I shrugged, and my uncle said nothing more until we left the café. "The way to find your friend's brother is to find Anoshkin's honeypot," he said as we walked back. "Something His Majesty's government would like to locate as well. And the way to the pot is to follow the diplomat or attaché with the right tastes."

I saw the conclusion. "And the way to find the target is to throw someone desirable into his path?"

"Exactly."

"Well, don't look at me. I have a face like a pudding." This was an even crazier scheme than his last one. I'd expected to troll the cafés, keep my eyes and ears open, and generally amuse myself at government expense. Clearly, I'd been too modest about my personal attractions.

My uncle sighed. "It would certainly be preferable if you had an angelic countenance, Francis. But needs must, my boy, and we can but try. Your being of age keeps us on the right side of the law. That's important here."

"How cheering to be legal," I said. "At home, I'm threatened with prosecution." Indeed, the more I thought about it, the less enthusiastic I was about government service of any kind.

"We'll knock a few years off your age," Uncle Lastings continued. "On a good day, I think you could pass for fifteen. Yes?"

"Hardly," I said. "I've just turned eighteen."

"Dim lights will help. You are to be out strictly after dark."

"Am I to be a rent boy or a vampire?"

My uncle laughed. "You have the family sense of humor," he said, then turned serious. "Neither. You are to be young and innocent, quite dazzled by Paris. Forget everything you learned in Berlin. And lose that knowing look."

"I think stupid is only attractive with an angelic countenance."

"True, but we must use what we have. Look young, Francis, and I think our man will bite."

I hoped not literally. "And do I know his name?"

"No, and neither do I. There are several candidates. For all I know, more than one may be involved."

"And if I am lucky, you'll follow them, and hope they lead us to Pavel?"

"Exactly. Though not me, personally. I am just an advisor."

Some advisor. "What happens then?"

"We detain our man for questioning and the Sûreté and the Deuxième Bureau take care of the rest."

What could go wrong? I could have compiled a list, but there was no time. We were due at a diplomatic reception that evening, and I had just time enough to change into evening dress. My uncle inspected the result before we sallied out.

"Yes," he said, seemingly quite pleased. "Formal dress is good. Definitely you could pass for sixteen, and if there are candles, fifteen is not out of the question."

I felt like an aging beauty.

"You are a young relative of our station chief. You will address

him as 'Uncle Horace.' I will point him out discreetly. We are not
related. In fact, you've never met me before, but I've been asked
to show you around. Understand?"

I understood that I'd probably have been better off as nephew
to a real British spy than to my uncle Lastings, even if, at the
moment, he looked not just respectable but distinguished. I
resisted the urge to ask if the small but important medals he'd
added to his jacket were his or just window dressing. I wanted
everything to go smoothly so that I could collect my other twenty-
five pounds and return to London. I could almost taste the fog.

Off to the embassy, a fancy pile of stonework with a fine garden in the back like the loveliest seaside hotel imaginable. I was
introduced to Horace, my newest uncle. He was tall and dry
and sandy haired with rabbity teeth and a glass eye that looked
considerably friendlier than his real one. He shook my hand and
exchanged glances with Uncle Lastings.

"Good to see you again, Francis."

"Nice to see you, Uncle Horace. This is impressive." No lie.
The entrance was big and marble clad and designed to intimi-
date. Empire architecture.

"Duty calls, but Lastings here will keep an eye on you. If you
need anything, ask him. Enjoy the evening."

I looked at Uncle Lastings, now the most casual of acquaintances. "First time in Paris?" he asked.

"Yes," I said, trying for naive enthusiasm. "A chance to try out
my French. I just started last year. Fifth form."

We went upstairs chatting as if we'd just met. I hadn't realized my unlamented time at boarding school would ever come

in handy. He escorted me to the reception room, a big salon lined in cream paneling touched with gilt, overhung by glittering chandeliers, and bordered by tall arched windows pouring in the evening light. Altogether too much light for my taste, too much of everything really. Roaming around the cafés was one thing. Trying to attract a pedophile at a diplomatic reception was quite another.

Nervous, I cast my eye on the drinks table, producing a subtle shake of the head from my uncle. Right: Schoolboys go for food first, and there was a fine array of pastries and biscuits of all sorts. Fortunately, I still have a schoolboy appetite. I selected a gateau slice with thick pink icing, and remembering that boys on school rations always take extras, I slipped some biscuits into my pocket.

"Aha! Caught you!"

I had a moment's fear that some café habitué was about to compromise me right out of the gate. I turned to see a bird-boned chap wearing a military uniform many decades out of fashion. He had thick white hair, a beaky nose, and amused blue eyes. "Keep you hungry, do they? Always did at Eton." He leaned closer, balancing on his silver-topped cane, and whispered, "I always take a few extra myself." He laughed, then nodded toward a tray of icing-topped fruit squares. "Fetch me a couple of those like a good lad."

I fixed a plate and held it for him, too, because despite his bright face and cheery air, he had quite a serious tremor. This was a nice old chap who pointed out some interesting pictures and told me more than I needed to know about his schooldays at Eton. Was he our target? I didn't think so, and even if he was, I didn't see him being able to do much harm. I was wondering how to get rid of him when a smart young embassy official came up, made excuses, and steered him away.

Was that suspicious? I watched them walk across the room toward a young woman wearing a short violet dress with a diaphanous shawl. She was our entertainment for the evening, all set to warble British art songs. Perhaps she was famous, for the old soldier seemed thrilled. He fluffed his feathers and kissed her hand with an eagerness that put me out of doubt. No honeypot for him, at least not of the sort we were seeking.

Songs, artful or otherwise, leave me cold, so I decided to visit the garden champagne table as preparation for the recital. Surely, a schoolboy on the loose would have at least one glass. As soon as I lost sight of Uncle Lastings, I went through the French doors to the perfect green velvet lawn outside.

Guests milling about, perfume and cigarette smoke and the dangerous breath of roses in the air. I set my course for a long, damask-covered table where I picked up a flute and happily discovered that the champagne was decent. I immediately felt better. A glass in hand is a great support if you're shy, which I am when I'm on unfamiliar ground.

I admired the roses with a stout lady in a vast red garden party hat—thinking I must describe it for Nan—and exchanged a few words with a slight and active waiter no more than my age before a very tall and handsome chap, blond with a perfect profile and a beautiful physique, strolled up to ask if I was having a good time. On a different occasion, his arrival would have brightened the whole evening. As it was, he was clearly embassy staff and so, strictly speaking, work.

"The refreshments are outstanding," I said. "And it is nice to speak English."

"Here to learn the lingo?"

"I started French at school, but it is not the same."

"Jolly well isn't. Though I had a French master who was excellent. He was a bit heavy with the cane, but his accent was perfection."

He went on in this vein. I learned about school theatrics— a conversational opening I might have taken but didn't dare— and about the amazing all-conquering rugby side of his last year, memories that made me wonder what it was about school that enchanted so many Englishmen. Ghastly food, bullying upper forms, brutal masters, ridiculous games, and cold showers: Had I escaped a taste for all that by being born in Ireland?

I feigned an interest in cricket to escape more talk of rugby, which, aside from all those bare legs and strong rumps, holds no attraction whatsoever. We ventured instead into a discussion of off spinners and googlies.

The man was a font of games knowledge, and sooner or later, I was going to flounder in athletic waters. But was this our man? Had he retained a passion for smaller boys along with their sports? I hoped that he was just a nice chap assigned to keep guests happy, because I wasn't picking up any signals at all, and I was relieved when he waved to someone across the lawn, wished me a happy time in Paris, and moved away through the crowd.

Guests were beginning to drift back into the embassy for the music. Uncle Lastings caught my eye as I crossed the main reception room to a salon decorated like a French king's bedroom and set up with rows of gilt chairs. I gave a little shake of my head. Maybe I was wrong, but I had detected only innocent, indeed, dutiful interest so far.

I took an aisle seat toward the back, intending a quick return to the champagne table. Up front, our soloist was introduced along with her pianist, a chubby fellow with a bald head and the face of an aging cupid. We were to have songs by Vaughan Williams, Delius, and Elgar, not the most enticing prospect for someone with a tin ear. I leaned back in my chair, prepared to be bored.

A tinkling introduction from the piano, before the singer, her hands held out to implore the Muse, her breath swelling her squarish chest, began Elgar's "Sea Slumber Song." She was barely through the first verse when I began to feel acutely uncomfortable. Music? Hard chair, too many sweets? The general unreality of visiting an embassy function to flush out a security risk? No, I decided, that was not it: I was being watched. And who could that be but someone who recognized me from the cafés? Possibly someone who knew me all too well.

That could be embarrassing. Worse, it could put my next installment of twenty-five pounds and a life in London in jeopardy. As casually as I could, I looked around. In the second row from the rear sat a distinguished-looking gent. Silver hair, silver mustache, silvery suit, possibly silver eyes for all I knew. Whatever he was, he looked solid sterling and top drawer, and he was focused not on the singer but on yours truly. I looked away, thankful I did not recognize him from Le Select, the Dôme, or the Parnasse Bar.

Applause, which I dutifully joined. Introductory chords from the piano and the soloist launched into another song. I was interested in the way her mouth moved, the ripple of muscle, the strong movements of her lips. Had anyone painted that? I wondered. And was I still under observation? I felt so. Like the handsome embassy official, I'd had some peculiar schoolmasters, one of whom had speculated that as a former prey animal, humans could sense even covert surveillance.

Another glance under cover of schoolboy restlessness. The distinguished gent was consulting the program. You're not the only pebble on the beach, Nan whispered in my ear, and I was about to assume I'd been mistaken when he raised his head and met my glance. I looked up at the ceiling as if suddenly interested in the stucco cornice decorations. Two songs later, I'd had enough. I slipped out of my seat and left the salon. I went to the French doors in the reception room but saw that the champagne table was already being cleared out on the lawn.

"Can I help you?" an official voice asked. It was a chilly voice, weighted with the arrogance of authority, and I wasn't surprised that it belonged to the man who'd been watching me. Seen close up, he had angry eyes set in a gleaming silvery perfection, marred only by the terrible shrapnel scar down the left side of his face.

"I was looking for the WC," I said.

"It's not out in the garden."

"I thought I might collect a champagne on the way." I smiled; winsome schoolboy was my brief after all.

He raised his head and frowned to show me what he thought of that idea; possibly he remembered no schoolboy pranks. "Entrance hallway. Gentlemen's is to the left," he said. "The rest of the embassy is out of bounds."

I thanked him, all on my best manners, but he stood and watched me as if I might be there to steal the silver or make off with the drapes. Or was something else behind his chilly anger? Did he intend to follow me and what was the best reaction then? I closed the WC door behind me and waited, but the marble floor outside remained silent, and when I returned to the performance salon, he was nowhere in sight.

CHAPTER TWELVE

I rode the Metro back from the embassy party. I assumed Uncle Lastings took a taxi, because he opened the door for me. He'd already lost his formal jacket and tie, rolled up the sleeves of his dress shirt, and opened a bottle of red wine. When I produced my reserve biscuits, he pronounced them just the thing.

"So," he said, "you got away with being a dewy-eyed schoolboy. I knew you could, my boy. You looked no more than fifteen." He patted me on the rump and added, "And a delectable fifteen at that. Formal dress suits you."

He was getting enthusiastic in a way I recognized from Berlin, and I was surprised to realize that I'd probably encourage him. Life with Uncle Lastings was complicated, but sex with him was not, whereas with Armand and Philip, life had been simple but sex was a business. Maybe I'd just needed a little perspective to see my treacherous uncle's virtues. Maybe. For the moment, I shrugged and stepped away. "No one much noticed me, if that's what you mean, except—"

"Nonsense," he said, still in a merry mood. "I saw you flirting with Willington."

"The handsome blond chap? He bored me with an account of his schooldays."

"I imagine he was a prefect and a star at everything. Plus you attracted Old Porter. Do you know, I think he served in the Zulu War."

"I can believe it, but he was slavering all over Miss Poole, the singer."

My uncle sighed. "Ah, Francis, you lack an appreciation for the female form. Miss Poole has a fine set of pipes and a beautiful case to keep them in." He threw back his head and laughed, so that even though I knew my uncle's catholic sexual tastes, I wondered if he was a bit drunk.

"In fact, there was only one person who made me uneasy."

I was wrong: Uncle Lastings was sober and instantly on the alert.

"I don't know his name, we didn't really talk, but he was staring at me during the recital." I described the man and relayed our brief conversation. "It doesn't sound like much," I admitted. Sitting with wine and biscuits in my uncle's comfortable flat, I thought I probably *was* acting like a nervous schoolboy until I saw my uncle's expression, all jollity gone. He made me recount every detail again and shook his head when I was finished.

"We could be down the rabbit hole." This is my uncle's shorthand for total disaster.

"I could be wrong. It's just I felt uneasy at his interest. And he *was* interested."

My uncle nodded rapidly. "I believe you, my boy. But why Stephen Byrone is interested, that's the crucial question. The possibilities . . ." Here he held up two fingers. "One, he's our man. That would be both awkward and dangerous. Two, he's not our man, but he's not been made privy to our scheme and now that he's found out about it, he's furious. That would be awkward and embarrassing."

"But why? What is he?"

"Stephen Byrone is the local head of the SIS."

I've always found multiple initials mean trouble.

"Secret Intelligence Service," Uncle Lastings explained. "The embassy provides diplomatic cover for a variety of intelligence officers."

"He didn't know that one of his people might be a target for blackmail?" Considering the fuss made about queers back home, that didn't sound terribly likely.

"Blackmail and corruption are always possible, and agents, even good ones, can become unreliable. There are certain pressures in the job." My uncle looked thoughtful. I knew he'd been with the Royal Berkshires, but now I wondered for how long and where he'd been posted afterward.

"We still need to find Pavel if he's alive. I promised Jules and Inessa."

"It's a mistake to make promises," my uncle said heavily. "Especially about events that are beyond your control."

"Are we going to run away, then?" I was angry. "Are you going to leave Paris and everyone and become someone else?"

My uncle put his hand on my thigh and winked. "No, I

intend to share some of *my* schoolboy reminiscences with you and clear my brain."

I hesitated just long enough to put him into doubt before I said, "Inspiration's where you find it."

"Indeed it is, my boy. And what I learned after hours at school has kept me entertained ever since." He laughed and put his arm around me affectionately, grabbed the wine bottle, and set a course for his bedroom, singing "A bit of what you fancy does you good," complete with high kicks, my uncle being a devotee of music halls of all sorts.

His school experiences were more entertaining than mine, even though mine got me expelled, and it was some time before we surfaced from the mess of rumpled sheets and pillows. Uncle Lastings shared out the last of the wine and fiddled with, but kindly did not light, one of his favored cigars.

"We do nothing for a few days," he said, his mind made up. "We may already have flushed him out; we must wait and see. I will find out if Byrone has discovered our plan. That will determine everything. In the meantime, you stay out of sight. It would be dangerous if anyone at the embassy but Horace made the connection between us."

I started to protest. I'd had enough seclusion.

"Just until the garden party at the embassy on Thursday. We will maybe make another sally then."

At least, I thought, we weren't *going over the top*, always his indication that things were taking a turn for the worst. In fact, my uncle seemed to have lost his sense of urgency, which gave me another idea. "I'm supposedly a schoolboy on a language course.

Is it plausible that I'd be working every minute? Or would I be out taking in the sights, visiting the cafés? Everyone knows the Parnasse Bar is a favorite with expats. And Jimmy, the head barman, he'd keep an eye on me, if you asked him, wouldn't he? If there was any sign of trouble?"

Now my uncle lit his cigar, a sign of deep thought, and it struck me, almost unwillingly, that somewhere in his devious mind he might be concerned for my safety. People are endlessly surprising, but I thought that was still too big an assumption to be relied on.

"You're known there," he said.

"Embassy staff do visit the Parnasse though?"

"Yes."

"Because it could be one of the others or someone I didn't meet at all."

"Quite right. But you'd have to be on your best behavior," he said. "If our man were to get something going with you, he might give Anoshkin's trap a miss. Remember that."

Though I doubted that I could hold a candle to Pavel's attractions, I promised anyway.

"An attack on two fronts?" My uncle considered this proposition and nodded. "But you wait a night or two. Let's see what we've stirred up first."

The next day, my uncle took me for a run to Dieppe in the van. I thought this was part of some plan, a rendezvous with Jules and Inessa, perhaps. I should have known better. He wanted to be sure that the paintings were properly loaded to be shipped across the Channel.

"We could have been looking for Pavel," I said on the way home. I was feeling anxious and guilty about the delay.

"All in good time," said my uncle. "I wanted to be out of Paris in case there were fireworks today at the embassy. It's always good to let the smoke clear."

That made sense, but back in the city, I asked him to drop me near Monsieur Chaput's detective agency. "He might have learned something."

My uncle was surprised—and seemed not best pleased—to learn I'd hired a detective.

"Well, technically not me. Jules paid for most of the work."

"I suppose there will be a bill," my uncle said drily.

"I suppose there will. Monsieur Chaput believes all the answers are in the documents."

"He'll be nothing but a damn paper pusher," said my uncle, but to my surprise, he parked the van a couple of blocks from the agency and walked over with me.

"Who are you?" I asked as we climbed the breath-catching stairs.

"I am your uncle. No, no, that won't do. I am your tutor. *In loco parentis* at the moment."

I rolled my eyes and knocked on the door.

We found Monsieur Chaput annoyed because there had been no word from Monsieur Dumoulin. "I understood that time was of the essence, that my client felt a real urgency," he said as he ushered us into his office.

"There was serious illness in his family," I said quickly. "He had to go north on short notice. My tutor, Monsieur Larouche, insisted we come to settle up with you."

Chaput sat down in his raised chair and relaxed a little. "The fee, of course," he said and slid a piece of paper across the desk. "But that is not the crucial thing. If the documents do not lie—and the French border control is very efficient—Bogdan Anoshkin recently entered Paris and secured a *carte d'identité* from the Paris Préfecture. He gave this address." Another piece of paper, which my uncle collected with considerably more eagerness than the bill.

"This does not necessarily mean he has rejoined the boy," Uncle Lastings said.

"Alas, no. And it does not give us reason to engage the police—yet. However, discreet inquiries might be made."

"Certainly," I said, but my uncle held up his hand.

"Not yet." He gave me a warning look. "I think a more oblique approach is needed. I would like to know who visits the residence, and I would like photographs of them. Can you arrange that?"

"Of course, monsieur, though it will be much more expensive than my work with the documents. Are we talking about an all-day surveillance? Or a twenty-four-hour watch?"

"Let us start with evenings, six to eleven, say, and go from there."

Monsieur Chaput thought for a moment and named a figure. My uncle must have been on expenses because he did not blanch. He pulled out his wallet, settled up our bill, and added a substantial retainer. "You can reach me anytime with a message to Jimmy at the Parnasse Bar." He added the number. "I will return any call as soon as possible. Usually within a half hour."

"*D'accord, monsieur.* That is very satisfactory." Monsieur

Chaput made as if to stand up, then paused and settled him-self again. "The residence is a most interesting one, over three hundred years old. It is one of the oldest private dwellings in the city."

My uncle looked nonplussed at this, and I was surprised myself. Was our target fond of antiques? Or had this rental noth-ing to do with a honeypot scheme? "An unusual choice," my uncle observed.

"Maybe," said Chaput, "maybe not." He smiled like a magi-cian about to produce the rabbit. "There are all sorts of stories about the house. One owner is supposed to have been involved in the assassination of Henry IV. Another is supposed to have been one of the frondeurs who opposed his son."

I thought that a Red commissar might feel right at home there and perhaps my uncle did, too, because he only shrugged.

Monsieur Chaput continued. "Alternately, the house is said to have belonged to one of the king's mistresses and to be con-nected to the Louvre via a tunnel. Of course"—he raised his hands to signal skepticism—"no one has ever found this tunnel."

"But the house is on the Left Bank?" my uncle asked in surprise.

"Correct. And doubtless that is why the tunnel has remained legendary. It would have to run beneath the Seine to reach the palace. Still, even a partial tunnel might be an asset—in certain businesses."

We could only agree that this was food for thought.

On our way back downstairs, I expressed my surprise that Uncle Lastings had hired the detective.

"I am known to all concerned at the embassy, so I could not stake out the building. The whole embassy staff must be under suspicion, so they cannot be asked, and Horace himself is too highly placed to be lurking around the rue Jacob. We need an outsider, preferably an obscure one, and Monsieur Chaput certainly fits the bill. Though," he added, "it will not hurt for us to have a look at this interesting property."

We drove by. The rue Jacob house was visible only as a series of steep slated gables behind the trees and high stone wall that surrounded what looked to be a large garden. Access was via the doors of a handsome iron gate with a fancy heraldic emblem, and a trip around the block revealed that the property extended to the next street.

"Very private," said my uncle thoughtfully. "And a quiet neighborhood."

"They'd notice cars, though."

"This is not a volume business," said my uncle. "This is a few discreet visitors."

"Making a difficult assignment for Monsieur Chaput?"

"He's charging enough. We'll see how ingenious he is."

We waited for the next several days. I received a delighted letter from Nan, who reported that she had chucked her situation and was already in London, sharing a bedsit with a friend and looking seriously at flats in Chelsea. I sent her a postcard of the Bois de Boulogne and a letter describing the Thursday garden party at the embassy, a dull affair of linen suits, flowered hats, and genial bores made tolerable only by the excellent champagne.

His Majesty's government clearly runs on the stuff. I ate a great many finger sandwiches and cakes and managed to drift away before the musical entertainment, a trio of clarinet, piano, and cello. No one propositioned me, no one regaled me with his school days, and except for a heavy-legged old dame who needed my arm to take a gander at the embassy roses, no one paid me the slightest attention.

Was that a good sign? I wondered. I returned to find the flat empty, and I was annoyed because I could have been out and about for half the evening with my uncle no wiser. But it was maybe not too late to take advantage of his absence. I hustled to change my clothes and I was almost at the door when my uncle returned, flushed and eager.

"I underestimated Chaput. He has been on the job and he has photos of several men, one of whom may be Anoshkin, one of whom he believes is English. We're going to pick up the evidence."

All right! Even a visit to dry Monsieur Chaput beat remaining in for the evening. Out front, I was surprised to see, not the van, but a dark Citroën.

"The van is known," Uncle Lastings said.

I was impressed. Somehow he had managed to tap into government money for an operation while simultaneously running his own dodgy scheme with one of the target's associates.

As on our previous visit, Uncle Lastings parked a few blocks from Chaput's agency. I noticed how he checked behind us and scanned the buildings all around, guarding his portable perimeter. I found this more amusing then than I would later.

Upstairs, one, two flights. On the third, he stopped to sniff the air and frowned. Then he took off, taking the steps two at a time. On the upper landing, we saw the door of the detective agency ajar. My uncle stopped and motioned for me to stay back. He edged toward the entrance, pushed the door open gently, and glanced inside. Then he gestured for me to follow.

The outer office was as we had last seen it, wooden chairs on either side of the rickety table. The inner office was another matter. The drawers of the file cabinets had all been pulled out, and folders and papers had drifted over the desk onto the floor. The green glass lamp was smashed, the desk chair overturned, and Monsieur Chaput lay next to it in a mess of shit and blood. My lungs contracted; I took a big gulp of the stinking air and wished I hadn't. My uncle was swearing softly but steadily.

"The photos?" I asked after a minute. I had a bizarre notion that he might want to make a search.

"They'll have gotten the photos." I took a step toward the desk and he added, "Touch nothing."

I nodded. "Who? Who did this?"

My uncle shrugged. "The Reds, possibly. Or whoever is corrupt at the SIS. Either way, we're down the rabbit hole, boy."

"Poor Chaput believed in documents," I said stupidly.

"He should have stuck to them. Come on. We were never here," my uncle added as we went on the stairs. "Never."

Out to the car. "Where are we going?" I asked.

"We need to let Horace know. We use Jimmy at the Parnasse Bar as a contact, but I'm not sure that is possible for me. I'd be spotted for sure if it's one of our people."

I felt that quite a lot of champagne would be needed to settle my stomach and take away the stench that lingered in my nose and at the back of my throat. "I could go," I said. "I was only the twice at the embassy, and the Parnasse is just the sort of place where an English student would drink."

My uncle gave me an appraising look. "You go in, you have a drink, you tell Jimmy the exact message I'll give you, and you take a taxi straight back to the flat. There's no playing about with these people, whoever they are."

"Absolutely. I could do with a drink."

I got another look. "One. You're just getting the evening off to a good start."

I nodded. I promised. For once, I had every intention of doing just what I was told. He dropped me a couple of blocks away, and if I hadn't felt both sick and shaky, it could have been one of the lovely evenings of my first days in Paris, strolling the boulevard and going between Le Select, the Dôme, the Dingo Bar, and the Parnasse. Same violet sky fading into a smoky lavender, same gaily lit cafés, dusty plane trees, and stars blooming overhead. Same laughter, same waiters in their long aprons, same painted girls—and boys.

But it was all I could do to walk straight. I tried to put thoughts of poor Chaput out of my mind, but he kept returning, bloodied but still in his overturned desk chair, killed for a handful of incriminating photographs. If a few pieces of celluloid had been enough to eliminate him, how much more vulnerable would Pavel be? It didn't bear thinking of.

I straightened my tie, rather askew, put my shoulders back as if my military father was still booming commands in my ear, and strolled into the Parnasse. Up to the bar. Lean a casual elbow. Why is it that nerves make even the simplest action seem not only complicated but implausible?

After a moment, I caught Jimmy's eye. I ordered champagne and asked if Horace had been in.

He shook his head, returned with a flute, and leaned over. "Photos lost," I whispered as I set the coins on the bar. "Detective shot dead. Advise Horace."

Jimmy's face never lost its professional, noncommittal smile, though he did say, "Perhaps monsieur would like a cognac?"

I shook my head and emptied the flute. I could have done with another and a cognac on top, but, mindful of my uncle's warnings, I turned away and almost bumped into a chap in a fine, pale linen suit and a handsome flat cap. Two beats and I realized it was Pyotr. Gone was the thuggish demi-apache look in favor of café society style. I should have had a lot of questions. Instead, I just said, "*Bonsoir.*"

"Francis!" He clapped me on the shoulder. "How good to see you." He gestured to Jimmy. "Two champagnes." A look at me. "Champagne, yes? See, I have not forgotten."

I protested I had to leave; I had an appointment, an assignation; I was already late.

"But there is always time for champagne," he said, and taking my arm, led me toward a table on the sidewalk, then returned to the bar for our drinks. If I'd really felt like myself, I'd have taken the opportunity to leave, courtesy be damned. But I was still shaky, and the thought of another restorative champagne was irresistible. I sat down and smiled at Pyotr when he returned, glasses in hand.

"To us," he said and we raised our glasses.

"I like your suit. You must have found a rich patron. Do tell."

Pyotr narrowed his eyes and shook his head. "I've found work. Of a sort."

He did not seem inclined to elaborate, and I was in no shape for any subtle interrogation. Pyotr was in a different mood. He wanted to know if I was still with the theater company. I was surprised and a little uneasy that he knew about that.

"*Tout Paris* knows," he said. "Friends of friends have seen the show with the beautiful Inessa. There are no women like Russian women." He raised his glass to the ladies of the fatherland.

"Inessa is superb," I agreed.

"And where is she now? *Tout Paris* wants to know."

I shrugged. "Ran away with a lover, I believe."

"You do not know?" He leaned across the table toward me, sounding incredulous.

"Why would I? She does not confide in me."

He leaned back in his chair. Despite his fine clothes and air of prosperity, there was still something feral in his expression. "Yet you were looking for her brother. It *was* her brother, wasn't it?"

Be careful, Francis, Nan said in my inner ear, but now I found it hard to come up with something ambiguous. Even an outright lie, such as I am normally good at, seemed well beyond my capacities. It was the shock, of course.

"It would be best if you told me, Francis. I have your interests at heart in this." Pyotr leaned forward and touched my arm. "Tell me!"

His face seemed to have dissolved on one side, an interesting visual effect. I'd seen nothing like it on canvas. I blinked, and the bright lights of the café darkened and shadows rose out of the street like goblins. I felt quite sick. I like alcohol, but drugs do nothing good for me. This was not the aftereffects of finding poor Monsieur Chaput and his scattered documents but the impact of some chemical that was overwhelming my system.

I knew that I had to get away from my treacherous friend. I pushed back my chair, but it was already too late. I swayed on my feet and Pyotr, quick as an eel, was out of his chair and around the table to put his hand on my arm. I shook it off, but with a laugh and a wave to the tables next to us, he put his arm around me and helped me onto the sidewalk. One step, two. I was going to be sick. I was going to fall. I was falling, no, being pushed, pushed into the open door of a large black car that had materialized amid the pedestrians and traffic and the laughter and music of the cafés.

"*Je suis désolé,*" Pyotr said and slammed the door.

With a terrific jolt, the car accelerated away, and my only consolation was that most of what I'd eaten over the last twenty-four hours landed in the lap of the heavy chap sitting beside me.

CHAPTER THIRTEEN

I must have passed out for a time, because I remembered nothing of the drive except that the man sitting in the backseat with me made a great fuss about his suit. Quite unfair. I hadn't asked to be shanghaied in a favorite café and taken on a fast ride in a swaying car, especially not when my head was reeling and my stomach rising. What did they want with me? And where was I? Lights and tree branches swept overhead. Traffic signals. Reflections. No sign of buildings, all gone. Vanished. *Tout Paris* had disappeared except for lights and trees. And cars. I was in a car, and there were others because I heard horns.

A jolt for a stop, causing my head to thump on what? Edge of the seat? A large shoe? I appeared to be lying on the floor of a car, and, yes, a shoe, attached to a leg, attached to some large being seated above me. Another jolt. Our driver had a heavy foot, unlike my last ride with—then a gap opened, a scary gap ending in darkness that was not interrupted until the car stopped, and there was a creak. A gate opening. We pulled forward onto a paved forecourt.

Car doors opening. My backseat companion stepped out, complaining loudly. Not English. Not French. I'd settled on Russian by the time the door on my side opened. My legs were seized, and I was hauled out like a dead fish. I felt rather like one, too. *Thump*, down on the pavement before a man silhouetted against the lighted door of the building. He was broad rather than tall, and his features were lost in the shadows. My stomach gave another twitch just the same. Something about him struck a chord and it was not a good one.

At his order, the driver and my angry backseat companion seized me under the arms and dragged me toward the house, a tall building with slated gables. A clatter behind us as the gate was closed. High walls, trees. Then lights and more darkness, but before my mind quite slipped away on its chemical excursion, I saw the face of the man giving the orders. I'd last seen him in a taxi outside the theater: Inessa's savior and Pavel's betrayer, Alexi. I was in for it.

Floor. I was lying on the floor. Unmoving. I was not in the car. Not in my uncle's flat. Not anywhere I recognized. The ceiling was a long way overhead, a chandelier dangling from the center. Off. The light was off, but it was not dark. Not completely. Grayish bars at the windows. Three windows with shutters. I sat up, my head spinning. My shirt was filthy, and my suit was probably ruined. I'd been at a café. Drinking champagne with—another blank—but it struck me that I'd had nowhere near enough money to drink to such excess. Something else must have happened, but I hadn't a clue.

I lay down again and perhaps I went to sleep because when the door opened, and Alexi, yes, it was definitely Alexi, came in and threw open one shutter, clear bright light poured in, bringing a glimpse of blue sky and the green tops of the trees. I was in an upper room.

Alexi said something to me in French, but *mon français* had taken its leave.

I started to shake my head and wound up back flat on the floor.

Alexi grabbed the front of my shirt and repeated his question, once, twice. Lots of sounds, lots of words, out of which all I understood was *Inessa*.

"Inessa," I said.

"*Où est Inessa?*" Alexi shouted.

His face was very close to mine, and I saw that his teeth were bad, his lips curiously red. When I couldn't answer, he slapped my face, dropping me back onto the floor. This was repeated several times, I think, for my sense of time had seemingly followed my knowledge of French and any memory of the previous hours.

"*Où est Inessa?*"

The penny dropped. He wanted to know where Inessa was. Now we were making progress. I shook my head. "Don't know."

He hit me in the ribs this time and I was aware of pain, but at a curious distance. He also said a great deal in Russian. I distinguished *Pyotr* several times. Pyotr was on his mind and not in a good way.

Pyotr was my pal who'd bought me a drink. My former pal who'd bought me a drink. Who'd apparently drugged me. Who'd apparently overdone it.

"*Où est Inessa?*" And this time he added, "*Avec Dumoulin? Eh? Jules Dumoulin?*"

I nodded and wished I hadn't.

"*Bien.*" He seized the front of my shirt again and shook his fist in my face. "*Et où sont Inessa et Jules?*"

"I don't know," I said in English and then, after a huge effort, "*Je ne sais pas.*"

He hit me a few more times, but the blows that knocked me back and forth produced nothing but faint nausea. "Claude," he said after a minute. Even with the drug, my heart jumped. Again, "Claude?" But his harsh voice was tentative, and I guessed that he did not know of the connection.

I shook my head and tried not to look relieved.

He cursed Pyotr and hit me, but I closed my eyes and dropped away into the darkness.

The next time I came to, I was very stiff, very sore, very thirsty. My head was pounding, my mouth was dry, and I had a great many bruises, but I could sit up. A moment later, I was on my feet in a dark, bare room. Well, not entirely bare. The one open shutter brought in a dim light, which might have been just before dark or just before dawn, to illuminate a large and ornate armoire, a straight chair, and a bed with no mattress, just springs. A spare bedroom.

I staggered to the window. I was high up, and there were no gutters or drainpipes or convenient branches. Even if there had been, I was not sure I would have attempted an exit. I hurt every-where, and I was still dizzy.

The door, then. I shuffled across and tried the handle. Locked, *naturellement*, as Armand would say. But French had returned along with the memory of Armand. And now I remembered that I had been sent to the Parnasse Bar to pass on a message via Jimmy. Sent by my uncle Lastings, alias Claude, and I knew that Alexi must not, on any account, learn that message or that Claude and I were related.

What time was it? I sat down by the window and listened. I may have dozed, because I did not hear the church bells start but gradually became aware of them. I counted to eight. At least eight, which meant it was night and late because dawn comes early this far north, and full dark comes late. Had I possibly been out for a day? If so, my uncle must know I'd come to grief. Would he and his embassy contact, Horace, do something useful about that? I couldn't begin to guess.

Where was Alexi? That thought brought a jolt of fear, fear of him and fear of what I might have said. He knew about Jules, probably had known about him for a while. He knew Jules's last name was Dumoulin, and a man of his talents would soon discover Jules's permanent residence. That meant danger for Madame Dumoulin. Who had to be warned. With this thought, I dragged myself to the window and looked down at a terrace with leg-breaking stone flags. No joy there.

The adjoining window presented the same problem, and the one on the side wall had been unhelpfully nailed shut. I pulled and rattled at it, until disheartened, as well as dizzy, I sat back down on the floor. I may have slept again, because the first thing I registered was a faint tapping. When I opened my eyes, the room was full dark. Another tap.

I got up and went to the door. "*Qui est là?*"

A silence, then a quiet scrambling and rattling in the lock before the door opened and a light blinded me so that I automatically stumbled back and raised my hands.

The light dropped and the door closed. I blinked. A blond boy stood before me with a flashlight in one hand and a large kitchen knife in the other. The knife occupied my mind right away but not to the exclusion of his face, which was wide and symmetrical with perfectly sculpted features. His eyes were dark like Inessa's and, yes, he could model for some Renaissance angel, but I leaned toward a St. Michael rather than an innocent cupid. He was almost as tall as I was and, though slim, he promised soon to be broad shouldered and powerful.

"*Pavel? C'est Pavel, n'est pas?*"

"You have been hurt," he said in slow but accurate English.

When I said "Alexi beat me up" in English, he gave a feral smile and stepped closer, the knuckles white on the knife hand.

"He wanted to know where your sister is." My voice was an appalling croak.

"My sister is dead."

"Your sister is very much alive, and she's in hiding with a friend of mine."

He shook his head. "She is dead," he said, so definitely that I wondered if Alexi could possibly have found her in the hours I'd been unconscious. Had I told him something crucial? I hoped not.

"If Alexi worked on you, you told him. Alexi can get anyone to tell anything." He spoke of Alexi's brutality with a mix of fatalism and pride.

"I don't know where she is hiding, and I couldn't have told anyway because they drugged me. I don't tolerate drugs well."

Pavel considered this.

"Could I have a drink of water?"

His eyes flickered uncertainly as if it was in his mind to cut my throat instead, but he turned and went out. I made a lunge for the doorknob; there was an answering rattle on the other side. The little bastard didn't have a key, but he was quick with some sort of lock pick. I sat down on the floor, my throat like sandpaper. I'd imagined a frightened, abused child. This was such a child grown strong.

A few moments later, the lock rattled again. The flashlight beam washed around the room, again momentarily blinding me, before Pavel dropped the beam. He handed me a glass of water that tasted better than the finest champagne, and, when I'd emptied it, a chunk of bread.

"Now prove my sister is alive."

I told him about the play, about Jules and his machines, about the way Alexi haunted the alley in a taxi every night afterward.

"That is Alexi," he said and nodded. I noticed that he still had the knife and I wondered that he was allowed a weapon.

"Inessa has been looking for you without Alexi's knowledge." I explained about hiring the detective and about his sudden and violent death. "That attracted some British embassy officials. That's why I am here. I was just taking a message when I was caught."

"You are English," he said, his face grim. I could see him waffling between hope of his sister's survival and the satisfactions of hatred.

"I was born in Ireland."

"Is that a difference?"

"A vast difference."

He moved his shoulders, then took out a handkerchief, wrapped up the knife, and slid it into his boot. "I came to kill one of the Englishmen," he said. "I thought it was my chance, now that the operation is finished."

"Finished?"

"Alexi and Anoshkin have their men." He held his hands up before his face as if pointing a camera. "They will blackmail them for their secrets. I hope they all hang."

"And you? What happens to you now?"

"Everything's to be wrapped up. They will kill me, probably as soon as Alexi returns. But I will take one of them with me." He gave me another feral glance. "Maybe you, too."

"Please remember that I'm only here because I was helping search for you. And that I can connect you to people who know where Inessa is. Forget about revenge, and let's get out of here."

He thought this over, fatalism fighting with what I had to admit was a slim hope. "The gate is guarded, and the wall is unclimbable. I know. I've tried." He raised his pant leg and showed me a nasty scar on his left shin. "They thought for a while I'd be no more use. But I healed up."

"And now you are running around armed in the middle of the night." I couldn't help sounding skeptical.

His smile was too sad and cynical for someone so young. "The guards can be bribed for anything short of escape," he said. "Not Alexi or Anoshkin, but the others. I amuse them and they close their eyes. But if they let us out the gate, Alexi would kill them on the spot."

"In the middle of Paris? In a house that can be connected to him?"

"He'd hide them." Pavel went to the window and gestured for me to follow him. "See that?"

In the grayish city light I saw a stone cylinder. "An old well?"

"He'd put them down there. That's where I'm to go, but Alexi will get a surprise." He patted the knife in his boot.

"Bodies in a well would stink to high heaven. How long before the neighbors would complain?"

He shrugged. "I just know what Alexi says when he is drunk."

I wondered if poor Monsieur Chaput's information could possibly be correct after all. "If this is the house Anoshkin rented—"

"Who else?"

"There is supposed to be a tunnel from the house right under the Seine. No one has ever found it, probably because the well must have had water in it. Is it dry now?"

Pavel nodded.

"Worth a look?" I asked.

He hesitated. "Is my sister really alive?"

"Yes. She looks like you, very beautiful, and she dances well and when she acts Human Hope in the play, the audience throws flowers to her."

He smiled for the first time. "You could not have made that up." He opened the door, and I limped out. He took a piece of metal from his pocket and fiddled with the lock until it clicked. "We will need some tools," he said and led me down the hall to a narrow back stair. At one point, he switched off the flashlight and motioned for me to be quiet. We crept past a room where someone was snoring gently. Pavel felt his way along the dark corridor to a closet near the kitchen.

He eased open the door and switched on the flashlight again. Cleaning supplies and tools. Wrenches, hammers, screwdrivers. He looked at me. I pointed to a stout steel pry bar and a large screwdriver. Pavel took the bar and handed me the screwdriver. He added a length of rope before closing the door softly. He lifted the latch on the kitchen door, and we climbed a short flight of stone steps to the garden.

The well was toward the back of a graveled courtyard, and our feet crunched on the stones. I froze, but Pavel took my arm. "They are all drunk except the two on the gate. And they will be half drunk."

Just the same, we tiptoed to the well, larger and more substantial than I had expected and closed off with a lattice of iron bars. Pavel shone the light between them. The bottom looked to be no more than six feet below, but no matter how he angled the light, we could not see if there was anything more to the hole.

"We must not waste the battery," he said, switching off the light.

We waited until our eyes adjusted to the dark before attacking the iron strips. The screwdriver broke on one that was secured by a bolt rather than a modern screw. "We need a wrench," I said, but neither of us cared to reenter the house.

Pavel put the pry bar under one strip and leaned his weight on it. Nothing. I added a hand. Still nothing.

I moved around the well, touching the metal strips until I

found one that was dry and flaky with rust. I beckoned Pavel, who slid the pry bar underneath the iron. We put all our weight and strength behind it, producing a screech that made us both start. Pavel froze and so did I, anticipating the guards' footsteps, their shouts and lights. When the silence continued, I felt under the bar. The fastener was loose and with a little effort, we pulled it out.

"We need two more," Pavel whispered.

Another search, another assault on the grill, another screech, more painful suspense. "They must think it's an owl," said Pavel. "I have heard them calling."

I wiggled the bar free, and we used it to lever one of the crosspieces. There was another frightful scraping and screeching but with that loose, the well cavity was open enough. We looked at each other. He was slimmer and would have fit easily, but I could see he did not trust me.

"I'll give it a try," I said.

Pavel helped me up onto the rim of the well, an operation that set all my bruises complaining. Grasping two of the remaining bars, I let myself down into the darkness. He switched on the flashlight so that I could see the sand and bricks below. I dropped farther than I'd expected and landed with a thud. "Let me have the light," I said, and he handed it down. Stone walls, some with moss, a strong smell of mildew, dust, and cobwebs. Debris underfoot. Some old boards leaned against one side. Leaves and twigs and small animal bones littered the floor. I ran the flashlight around the wall that seemed solid everywhere, and I was about to say I'd been wrong when I hear the toot of a horn, a shout at the gate, the sound of a car crunching over gravel.

"Alexi's back," Pavel hissed. He dropped the pry bar to me, scrambled onto the rim of the well, swung his legs over the opening, and jumped down beside me. "He will search the house first." He held his hand out for the flashlight. "Now, where is this passage?" His tone was threatening.

I shook my head, but the sounds of voices moving toward the house lent urgency. I began pulling away the boards and patting the stones beneath, though I had a sick feeling that the idea had been ridiculous from start to finish.

"They will see that the grate has been opened. They will shoot us like rats." He took out the knife, and I thought, *Good-bye, Nan.* I was wondering if Uncle Lastings would find out what had happened and let her know, when Pavel turned and stuck the blade between two stones. Then between another and another. "Give me a hand. This stone is loose."

I found the pry bar amid the leaves and mess on the floor of the well and inserted it behind the stone. A jerk, another, and the stone, which proved to be no thicker than a brick fell out and bounced off my foot. At that moment lights went on overhead, illuminating what looked to be a rotting wooden door behind the stonework.

"Quick, quick! They've found we're gone," Pavel said in a tight, frightened voice. "They can light the whole garden."

I put the pry bar to the next stone and the next, and Pavel grabbed the loosened stones and pulled them away, revealing a small door, cracked and splintered and rotted at the bottom but locked.

"Hold the flashlight." Pavel fished the pick from his pocket.

He started on the lock, but the old mechanism was so unfamiliar there was not even a rattle.

"It's rusted out," I said.

I put down the flashlight, lifted the pry bar, and inserted in near the lock. As the ancient iron nails groaned in the wood, footsteps crunched on the gravel faster and faster. In desperation, Pavel grabbed the loosened board and threw himself backward. The wood, rotten for most of its length, came away. We thrust our weight against the rest of the door, and it collapsed, tumbling us into a low, dank opening. Pavel grabbed the flashlight and switched it off just as someone reached the well above.

"Pavel?"

He shrank back against me.

"Pavel?" Whoever it was touched the loosened bars of the grate. Without understanding a word of Russian, I knew from the man's wheedling tone that he'd guessed where Pavel was and was persuading him to come out. Down below, we hardly dared to breathe.

Whoever it was now rattled at the grate—he must have been too big or too heavy to squeeze through the opening—and his voice, formerly cajoling, turned harsh and violent. Threats come through remarkably well without translation. A hoarse shout of, "Pavel!" Once, twice, before his voice dropped to a whisper, an appeal. I sensed a complicated relationship before we heard his footsteps retreating. Pavel said nothing, and I didn't ask. He turned on the flashlight, revealing that we were at the mouth of a tunnel no more than four feet high. The footing was damp, the walls dubious, the floor sloping down into a murky claustrophobic darkness.

I looked at Pavel, and I think neither of us would have chanced it if we hadn't heard footsteps again. Multiple footsteps.

"Pavel?" someone said, before something bounced off the grate and into the well, followed by a thunderous blast that sent us both tumbling and somersaulting and slithering down the tunnel.

CHAPTER FOURTEEN

Darkness and dust. I sat up coughing and choking, only to knock my head against a piece of wood. Everything was silent. This was it: I was dead and buried. Then I moved one arm and understood I was alive. But my legs were immobilized, so, though I was not dead, I was nonetheless buried. Buried in such utter, paralyzing darkness that for a moment I was consumed by panic and started wheezing and gasping. I was well on my way to disaster when I saw a faint round light just a few feet away.

I thrashed my legs and wriggled out of the dirt to make a lunge for the light. I touched a flashlight, solidly metallic and real. I wasn't in a grave after all. I was in the tunnel. The tunnel from the well. With Pavel.

"Pavel? Pavel, are you there?" Just the silence, a peculiar ringing silence. Yes, there had been a blast, an explosion, and Pavel and I had been blown into the tunnel. "Pavel!"

I got up on my hands and knees, knocked my head again, and fell over something both firm and soft. "Pavel!" He gave a groan, and I shined the light on him. His face was spattered with earth and his eyes were dazed, but I saw no blood. No bones at odd angles, either. His lips moved without producing a sound. Or, rather, whatever sounds he made, I could not hear. And it appeared, he could not hear me, either, for he touched my arm and then his ear.

The blast, of course. I got to my knees and swung the light around. Ahead was the black mouth of the tunnel sloping down who knew where; behind, a heap of earth and stones where the walls of the well had collapsed. I clawed my way up as far as I could and began pulling away the debris, but I couldn't get any purchase on the earth, and I couldn't begin to make way through the stones now jumbled in an unstable pile.

I slid back down and sat, turning off the flashlight to save power. I don't know how much time passed before I heard Pavel say, "Which way?" and realized that I could hear, if faintly and through a peculiar ringing in my ears.

"I couldn't move any of the debris," I said.

Pavel had a go just the same, scrambling and digging like a terrier after a rat. Finally, he backed down the pile. "What time do you think it is?"

"No idea."

"They will think we're dead. They'll have gone," he said.

That was certainly possible, and buoyed by the idea, we began working together to shift the pile. But the combination of heavy clay soil, old wood, and massive stone blocks soon discouraged us, especially since we had difficulty telling which way we should be digging. The old dust and mold got my asthma going, and Pavel alone was not strong enough to move the larger stones. We were worried, too, about the flashlight batteries giving out, and at last we decided to chance the tunnel.

We had to proceed bent nearly double. If some randy king had made the trip regularly, he must have been a midget. We took turns leading the way, feeling along the dank and chilly walls, our flashlight sending a hopeful round circle ahead of us. Down, the tunnel led down, and soon it was wet underfoot. At first just dampness, then mud that sucked at our shoes and pulled at our legs. Once we startled a rat. Pavel jumped and started swearing in Russian, but I was relieved. Unless the rodent had been trapped with us by the blast, the tunnel must come out somewhere.

I walked in front after that, splashing through puddles below, sprinkled by chilly drips from above, and trying to forget that the Seine might actually be running overhead. Pavel began to hum in a high, frightened voice. "Miners do this all the time," I said, but I'd never fancied being a miner, and I don't think Pavel had either. Soon my back was aching as if cracked in a dozen places, and my legs were cramping up from the strain. We heard a nasty splashing sound and before we knew it, we were over our knees in water.

Pavel stopped. "We're going to drown," he said.

I raised the flashlight. We were approaching a flat black puddle of unknown depth, but beyond—"Look," I said. "It rises. The tunnel starts to rise."

Pavel agreed it did, but he refused to budge until I said I would go first and left him with the flashlight. "Keep it on the water," I said and he nodded.

I waded into the puddle, mucky and slimy on the bottom.

Ankle deep, knee deep, thigh deep. I slipped once and had to thrust a hand to the dubious bottom to keep my face out of the foul water. I floundered forward, fell onto my knees twice, but then, yes, a surface and not dirt, stone. And not just stone but stones sloping up, almost a ramp.

"Come on! There's a stone floor here. Throw me the flashlight when you get in too deep."

He hesitated only a moment before wading in cautiously. Halfway through, he started to slip and slide, our only light swinging up and down and side to side, but he refused to let it go until the water reached his waist. Then, instead of throwing the flashlight to me, he stuck it in his teeth and slogged across like a pirate. Drenched and muddy, we rested for a moment before starting up the stone-lined passage. Wet as we were, we slipped and fell on the rounded stones, especially after our flashlight began to waver and fade, and we had to feel our way along the walls.

But the air was better, the ceiling higher. And the floor was dry, so that I was sure we had dry land above us. But where? The passage narrowed and then, to our shock, ended abruptly. We were in a stone cul-de-sac, no, not entirely stone, brick. The passage had been bricked up. I could feel my chest tightening, but Pavel took out the knife that had survived our trip safe in his boot and began testing the mortar.

"It is crumbling," he said, and after a moment, he'd knocked one brick free. Immediately there was a draft, the damp and moldy air of the tunnel refreshed. Though we cut our fingers and scraped our knuckles, it was not long before we had removed half a dozen bricks. I gave Pavel a boost, and he wriggled through the opening.

I passed the flashlight through the hole and he said, "A cellar. We're in some big cellar."

He found a stout piece of wood and told me to stand back. A dull thud, another, and an irregular lump of bricks detached and fell at my feet. I scrambled through the opening and stood up on a stone floor. Pavel turned the light so that I could see the outline of what appeared to be the base of a huge tower. Built of large, well-cut stone blocks, it reached the ceiling, and was so impressive that Monsieur Chaput's story might be true after all: We could be in one of the lower levels of the Louvre.

"There must be a staircase," I said. "We need to get to a floor with windows before our flashlight gives out."

We followed the curve of the stonework, picking our way among building debris and mysterious holes, piles of earth, rock outcrops, and ancient pillars. Our dying light cast immense shadows, accompaniment to the hollow sounds of our feet on the flagstones. We walked on and on without finding any stairs or any door until suddenly we were in pitch darkness.

I heard Pavel shake the flashlight, trying unsuccessfully to nurse a little current from the batteries. Then silence. We would have to feel our way forward, and there was an excellent chance that we would wind up walking in a circle. For a few minutes, we stood still, uncertain of how to proceed and frightened of falling into one of the rocky ditches that must have been fragments of a long dry moat. We could easily be badly injured in one of them, and if we were, we might die without anyone knowing.

"We could call," said Pavel.

"If this is the Louvre, it will be closed for the night."

"You do not have a watch," he said in an accusatory tone, as if this was a great failing on my part. "All the Englishmen had watches. The Frenchmen, too."

"I'm not a diplomat, and I can't afford a watch."

He seemed set to sulk about this for I heard him move away, then he reached back to touch my arm. "Francis!"

I turned toward the sound of his voice. "A light!" he said. "Isn't that a light?"

There was a horizontal streak no wider than a pencil, a glimmer so faint it had been lost even in our weak flashlight beam. "A door?"

"Yes!" He started forward eagerly, and I caught his shoulder.

"Careful. It won't do to fall now."

We put our hands against the rough stonework and edged forward. Several times we kicked against protruding stones and barked our shins on unseen boulders, but at last Pavel exclaimed, "There are steps. Steps going up."

We felt our way toward the streak of light that, oh yes, issued from under a door. Pavel ran his hands over it and said, "Give me room."

I heard the rattle of his lock pick. Whoever taught him knew the trade well, because it was not very long before I heard a click, followed by the sound of the doorknob turning and a protesting creak from long disused hinges. I put my shoulder to the door and with our combined weight it swung open. We'd reached a long corridor. Pipes and wires ran along a ceiling lit by a few bare hanging bulbs. Pavel closed the door behind us.

"You look a fright," he said.

I returned the compliment. We were filthy from head to foot, our clothes soaked and ruined, our shoes caked with earth, our hands and faces muddy. Worse yet, we left a track of earth and water wherever we stepped. We needed to clean up enough to avoid attention and we needed to find out the time.

Down the corridor. Curious as a cat, Pavel rattled every door and poked his head in all the unlocked ones. Finally, we found the janitor's room with a sink and water. We washed our faces and hands, wiped our shoes, and wrung out our sodden pants, an operation that revealed an assortment of tears and rips. I was wondering if we could possibly dry them when Pavel walked over to a set of hooks and lifted down a pair of the blue coveralls French workers wear.

"Is there another one?"

Pavel threw me the pair he was holding and lifted another from its hook.

They were faded and worn and smelled of sweat and hard work and were absolutely perfect. Wearing these and carrying a broom or a shovel, one could come and go as easily as the Invisible Man. We put them on over our shirts, rolled up our ruined pants and jackets, and thrust them into a waste bin. I picked up a broom, and Pavel took a dust shovel. Thus protected, we wandered the vast basement until we located a set of stairs. These were unlit, and we climbed slowly in the darkness, occasionally stumbling when we came to a landing. At last we reached a set of double doors and pushed them open.

We were in the palace proper. The room was a king-size hall, long enough for all his knights and all their horses, too, with a row of tall, arched windows that brought in the grayish light and the faint glow of the night city. The ceiling was lost in shadows high overhead, and the walls were lined with the dim and mysterious shapes of ancient sculptures, one of which, graceful, armless, draped from the hips down, I recognized immediately: *Venus de Milo*. We were certainly in the Louvre, and I knew exactly where we were in the immense building.

The next thing was to find an office, somewhere with a clock, somewhere with lights. It must have taken us over an hour, but after walking miles of wood and marble floors and crouching behind statues or display cases anytime we heard a night guard on his rounds, we found ourselves in a corridor with what appeared to be office doors. The whole place was only dimly lit, but Pavel did not need much light to work his magic. The second door he unlocked proved to be equipped with a telephone and a clock. It was exactly two A.M. when I rang Uncle Lastings.

He listened without interrupting. When I had given a semi-coherent account of our adventures and appealed for protection for Madame Dumoulin, he asked if we could get out of the museum without being detected.

I said that thanks to our workers' coveralls we could easily leave after the museum opened. "Before that—I'm not so sure. There are a number of guards, and the doors may have alarms."

"They will probably be locked from the inside as well," he said.

"Locked has not proved to be a problem."

He thought for a minute, then said, "How long will it take you to get out?"

"Unless I've gotten turned around, we're down in the service areas of the long building facing the Seine, and the Porte des Lions at the west end is probably our best bet."

"I'll drive along the river in an hour," said my uncle. "Look for the green van. I'll do two passes. If you're not there, I'll assume you can't get away until the museum opens."

I replaced the receiver. "Let's go," I said. "We haven't a lot of time."

We switched off the light and, when the corridor remained silent, slipped out. Most of the hallways were badly lit, if lit at all, and we made several mistakes that took us into the dead ends of offices and conservators' studios. On the other hand, we felt quite safe, as we'd seen no guards since we descended to the service level. When we reached what we thought must be the end of the vast wing, we started to search for stairs, a process that turned out to require a good deal of backtracking.

At last we located the way up and climbed as fast as we dared in the pitch darkness of the stairwell. The first doors we reached gave onto another set of subterranean rooms and corridors. Back to the stairs, which besides being dark, were extremely hot and close. We reached fancier doors after the second flight and opened them to the welcome sight of the gray Parisian night behind impressive windows. But this was not exhibition space, and to our dismay, we found that it was chopped up into offices and storage rooms without any clear pattern.

"There should be a door on the river side," I told Pavel. We made sure we had reached the west end of the building, then started searching. Down one corridor, then another, passing dead

ends, locked hallways, and temporary partitions that looked to
be permanent, before we saw an open hallway. Thank you, Louis
Whatever! No little side doors for the kings of France! We were
ready to run for it when the unmistakable scent of Gauloise hit
my nose. I held out my arm, and Pavel stepped hastily behind
one of the omnipresent cabinets that seemed to hold another
museum's worth of art in reserve. Guards taking a break from
their rounds were smoking in the hall.

I sat down on the floor beside Pavel and we waited. I could
almost hear the minutes ticking off. *Please let them finish their
vile cigarettes and get back to work!* But the men seemed in no
hurry. Once in a while, we heard a vehicle passing along the road
that skirted the Seine. Was one of them Uncle Lastings's van? It
couldn't have taken a whole hour to get this far, could it?

A bell sounded on the night wind. One, two, three. I held my
breath, but there was no fourth peal. But it was time—we'd have
to do something. I was wondering if we would have to retreat to
a lower level and try another entrance, when, with what sounded
like jovial good nights, two of the men were sent out the door by
what must have been their replacements.

We waited until all was locked up again and the guards had
begun their respective rounds, one of them making a cursory
pass through the corridor where we were hidden. When he had
returned to the main hallway and his footsteps faded on the stairs,
we crept out to the entrance. The good thing was that there were
some steps between the hallway and the doors. Once crouched on
the bottom step so that Pavel could go to work, we were out of
sight of anyone on the stairs or even passing through the corridor.

"Quick as you can," I said nervously.

Pavel swore softly in Russian but otherwise didn't answer. The rattle of the pick seemed very loud, and I could not keep myself from creeping up the steps every other minute to be sure no one was around. Clearly this mechanism was so old as to be completely unfamiliar, because Pavel's vocabulary grew more and more ornate: French kings did not skimp on security.

A bell somewhere. Tolling the quarter hour?

Just then Pavel said, "*Bien!*" and stood up. He turned the over-size doorknob and the door swung open. I leaped for the sidewalk, and Pavel shut the door and rattled the pick in the lock. That boy was a craftsman.

The vast building loomed over us, but we were outside at last and aboveground. Never had a cloudy city sky looked better, nor the faint scents of exhaust, river, and drains been more welcome. We'd been saved from bombs and drowning and suffocation and psychopaths. Just the same, the fear I'd felt in the tunnel lingered as a twitchy anxiety. We were standing vulnerable on a major street. Could Alexi or one of his confederates be driving around? Could we be spotted by them? Or questioned by some suspicious gendarme? Had we missed my uncle? Had he come and gone? And would he find us if he hadn't? I was on tenterhooks until I spotted slow-moving headlights. I stepped out of the shadows to the curb. Was that the van? Yes!

"Hurry, Pavel!" I called.

Just then lights burst on in the hallway of the Porte des Lions. Pavel jumped back from the door and leaped down the steps.

The van stopped with a squeal. The passenger door opened, and Pavel and I squeezed into the front seat beside Uncle Lastings, who put the van in gear and his foot on the gas.

CHAPTER FIFTEEN

Uncle Lastings kept his foot down all the way to Madame Dumoulin's village, screeching around the sharp bends of narrow French lanes and blasting through crossroads. Fortunately, it was still before dawn, and there was no traffic, although he did have to brake for the occasional string of cows being driven in for milking or to avoid early farmhands on their way to sheds and stables.

He made us go over the events of the evening and all the questions Alexi had asked. Beyond the fact that he was looking for Inessa, I was quite hopeless.

"I said she was with Jules, but he already knew that. And he must have known Jules's surname, because there were stories in the press. He could easily have found out where Madame Dumoulin lives."

"But obviously he hadn't found her yet. You're sure you didn't tell him?" my uncle demanded. He seemed to feel that I had let down the side in a big way.

"I was semiconscious," I said.

My uncle was all focused and military, which gave me insight into what he had been before he embarked on frauds of one sort or another and took to changing his identity. He was a slippery character, but I hoped that his present air of decision and competence was genuine.

Pavel proved to have far more useful information. He knew a lot about Alexi, having studied his habits right down to the make of his car and the caliber of his handgun. "He's a night bird," Pavel concluded.

My uncle swore at this. The Russian would surely have a head start on us.

"Oh, yes. If he knew where my sister was, he would go right away."

"And you're sure he left?"

"He'd hardly have stuck around after that explosion," I said.

"So you must have told him something useful," Uncle Lastings insisted. "Otherwise, why didn't he leave before?"

"I don't know. I can't handle drugs."

My uncle started on about the folly of drinking with Pyotr then broke off abruptly to ask Pavel if he thought Alexi would go alone or take some men with him.

Pavel thought this over and shook his head. "He told Vlad and Taras nothing except their orders. Everything was supposed to be in the service of the fucking revolution, so he would not have wanted them to know about Inessa." Pavel bit his lip, his face white and strained. "He might have told me that she was alive. He might have told me that."

"He told Inessa nothing about you, either," I said. "She

knew nothing until we learned that you had come into France with Anoshkin."

"I will kill Anoshkin." Pavel was assembling quite a list.

"Get in the queue," my uncle said.

To my dismay, he planned to go directly to where he'd hidden Jules and Inessa. "What about Madame Dumoulin and Luc? I still don't know where you put Jules and Inessa, but I'm guessing you told Madame Dumoulin. Alexi would figure the same."

"With luck, he'll find us waiting for him," my uncle said, as we roared around yet another sharp bend.

"But they could be killed! Or badly hurt—whether they are willing to tell him anything or not. And if they don't tell him right away, he could still be there. At this hour he might not even have found the house yet."

I kept this up until my uncle agreed. He was skeptical but cautious, first driving past the house, then, after making sure there was no one around, pulling out of sight next to the barn. I climbed over Pavel and got out, my legs shaking.

Up the step, knock on the door. No response. *It's past four in the morning. What did you expect?* Again. Nothing. I tried the handle. The door was unlocked. "Madame Dumoulin! Luc!" I called and called again. No answer, but suddenly I heard a rustling and thumping down the dark hallway. I shouted for my uncle before groping my way to the kitchen where two dark shapes lay on the floor. "Madame Dumoulin!"

The shape moved, twitched. I felt for her face, expecting blood, but found a rag tied over her mouth. I was so nervous my fingers slipped on the knot, and I had to go to the big block of knives to get one to cut the gag. She gasped and choked and cried, "Luc! Is Luc all right?"

He was banging his feet on the floor. Stumbling over her legs, I reached him and cut his gag. By this time Uncle Lastings and Pavel had arrived, and Pavel's big knife made short work of the ropes that had trussed up my friends. Madame embraced Luc, who was fighting back tears, then lit the gas lamp. We saw that her face was badly bruised, both eyes blackening. Luc had a swollen lip and a nasty, oozing cut on one cheek.

"Who did this, Madame Dumoulin?"

She shook her head. "No one we knew. He must have gotten in through a window. I woke up and there he was. He was very strong but short with dark hair and eyes like a cat."

"That's Alexi," said Pavel. "And he carries a knife." Automatically, he leaned down to touch his own weapon, safe again in his boot. I guessed that he had picked up quite a few habits from his ruthless protector.

"He wanted to know where Jules was!" Madame Dumoulin's voice was anguished.

"Did you tell him?" My uncle's voice was rough with anxiety.

Poor Luc went white. "He threatened Mama," he said, his eyes streaming. "He promised he would kill Mama."

"Oh, *bien sur*, he certainly would have," said Pavel, who patted him sympathetically on the shoulder. "No one escapes Alexi."

"There is no time. We have to go. Get help from one of your neighbors," Uncle Lastings told Madame Dumoulin.

"And the gendarmes?" Madame asked.

My uncle hesitated. "If we could have an hour?"

"It will take that long to reach the station," she said. "There is no phone except in the café and that will still be locked."

My uncle nodded and hurried down the hall. I hated to leave, but Madame almost pushed us out the door. "Hurry!" she said.

We ran for the van. "The boy stays behind," my uncle said.

I jumped in and slammed the passenger door, but, forewarned, Pavel was too quick. As we reversed down the drive, I heard the rear door of the van bang shut. Uncle Lastings swore but did not stop. Into first, into second, into third, we careened down the narrow road. He at last told me where we were going—a small farm nearby that Madame owned. Though a neighboring farmer leased the land, the house had recently become vacant. I'd once accompanied Jules when he collected the rents, and between the two of us, we found the place quite easily even though it was hidden behind a wall and a tall hedge. A narrow unpaved track led from the country road to the single-story stone farmhouse, quiet and private and possibly a trap.

Uncle Lastings stopped on the shadowed verge. We stepped out to morning birdsong and rattling insects. Through the morning mist, we saw the low stone house fronted by two fine chestnut trees. Parked out front was a black car that Pavel recognized immediately as Alexi's.

My uncle nodded and gave the orders. "You two will stay on the perimeter. You, Pavel, just behind the gate, watch for anyone arriving. Francis, take the barn. They could be there, if—" He didn't finish the thought and didn't need to.

He took out his Webley and, showing a better turn of foot than I'd expected, sprinted along the hedge so that he could

approach the house from behind a pasture fence. I moved into
the shadows of the chestnut trees and crouched a moment in the
long, wet grass before making my way toward the barn and the
stable. I'm not fond of either even under the best circumstances.
Horses make my eyes water and swell up; hay riles my asthma.
At that moment, I also had to resist imagined images of injury
and carnage. I told myself that the car meant Alexi was still on
the scene. Had anything terrible happened in the barn, he would
already have decamped.

With this in mind, I entered the open door. And sneezed vol-
canically. Mistake! I shrank against the cobwebby interior wall,
my heart hammering, and it took a moment before I realized that
the sound could not have carried to the house. I stifled another
sneeze just the same before looking around. Hay was stacked to
the roof on either side, but the floor between was bare, without
any trace of blood or violence—or any sign of my friends.

Breathing shallowly to thwart the dust, I went over to the
stable. I looked in each stall but found them empty. Obviously
the farmer employed his own animals. Everything was so quiet
and ordinary that I figured my uncle had given me the job to
keep me out of the way.

Between the stable and the house, a ragged clump of lilacs
provided cover, and with my nose streaming from the hay, dust,
and dander of horses past, I moved through them. When I was
within a few yards of the house, I saw a faint light in the front
room. I crept toward the window and risked a glance. In the
light of the oil lamp, I saw Jules was tied to a chair. He had blood
on his face and on his shirt, but he was conscious and clearly

furious. Inessa's hands were bound behind her, and Alexi, who had an ugly-looking pistol with a long narrow barrel, was speaking loudly and urgently to her in Russian.

Inessa kept shaking her head until Alexi stepped up to Jules and put the pistol to his head.

She gave a shriek. He turned at the sound, and I ducked. More conversation in Russian followed. I guessed that Alexi was making her an offer for Jules's life, and her expressive voice, high and despairing, told me that the price was a painful one.

I risked another glance before a rustle nearby nearly sent me running. Uncle Lastings beckoned me across to the other side of the door, where we would both be hidden when it opened. I crouched beside him, very conscious of my noisy breathing and galloping heart, which had not slowed one bit before the door opened.

Inessa stepped out, weeping, with Alexi right behind her. But he'd made a mistake, one I realized with a start that my uncle had counted on. Secure in his triumph, Alexi had holstered his pistol, and before he could turn to close the door, Uncle Lastings struck his head with the Webley.

"Run, Inessa!" I shouted.

She leaped away despite her bound hands, but as soon as she realized that Alexi was on the ground, she lunged back into the house to Jules. My uncle deftly lifted Alexi's pistol from his shoulder holster, snapped a pair of handcuffs on him, and hauled the unconscious Russian into the house. "Go fetch Pavel," he said.

I ran down the drive toward the road, calling in relief and excitement, "Come quick! Inessa is safe!"

He bolted up the drive faster than I could manage. By the

time I got to the house, Pavel was locked in his sister's arms, Jules was untied, and he and my uncle were discussing Alexi, who was lying, still dazed, on the floor. Jules was all for bundling him into the car and driving straight to the gendarme station.

This didn't suit my uncle for a number of reasons, and he changed the subject as soon as he saw me. "You might have brought up the van," he said, before I reminded him that I can't drive.

He gave me a haughty look as if I was his unsatisfactory batman, but in the delay, he had made up his mind. He handed Jules Alexi's sidearm and told him to take the van with Inessa and Pavel. "Keep going," he said. "Let your sister know you're all right and clear out." Then, seeing Alexi stir, he steered Jules to the door for more quiet advice. I saw my friend nod. He shook hands with my uncle before embracing me. "*Merci bien*, Francis."

Inessa kissed me in turn. Pavel clasped my shoulder, and after a quick, unreadable glance at Alexi, he handed me his knife. "In case you need it," he said, touching my shoulder again before my uncle hurried them away. We watched from the doorway, and Uncle Lastings didn't relax until we heard the van toot at the end of the drive.

"What now?" I asked.

My uncle shrugged and held out his hand for Pavel's knife. He wrapped the blade in a handkerchief before slipping it in a pocket of my coveralls. He lowered his voice. "I expect Horace very soon. I hope before the gendarmes arrive. They could be awkward."

"Why can't we take Alexi with us and turn him over later? Or leave him here?" Tranquil pastoral scenes have always spelled trouble for me, and I very much wanted to be away. "We could take his car, couldn't we?"

"It would be better to have Horace pick us up and leave Alexi's vehicle as a little mystery for the gendarmes." Nonetheless, my uncle consulted his watch and frowned.

Behind us we heard motion, Alexi struggling to his knees. Just then, a car came up the drive. "Ah," said my uncle. "All is tickety-boo. That will be Horace. He can take charge of Alexi, and you and I can disappear."

He went eagerly to the door, but when he opened it, I saw his back stiffen.

"Stephen," he said.

I caught a glimpse of silver hair, scarred face, upright carriage—all last seen at the embassy recital. This was bad. I glanced toward the back of the house, and I may even have taken a step in that direction, because I admit I was tempted to abandon my uncle and make a quick exit. A burst of angry Russian from Alexi stopped me.

Stephen Byrone, he of the silver hair, heavy presence, and uncertain loyalties, answered fluently before casting a chilly eye on yours truly. "Who is this boy, Lastings? And what is he doing here."

"A victim of a kidnapping. I really should say of a shanghaiing. Once he was freed, I could not safely leave him behind."

Another burst of Russian. No doubt a different account from Alexi's perspective.

"And the other boy?" I sensed that Byrone was trying for indifference and not quite managing. "This—Pavel Lagunov? Where is he?"

I expected more Russian, but when Alexi was silent, I said, "The blond boy? He's dead."

My uncle gave me a look but didn't contradict me. More surprisingly, neither did Alexi.

"He was caught in the explosion. The tunnel collapsed. We should both have been killed, but I got away." In the tunnel and in the Louvre and with all the excitements afterward, I'd managed to forget that or at least keep it to the back of my mind. Now it was front and center. I remembered the shock of the explosion, the clouds of ancient dust and mildew, the black unwholesome pools, the Seine running overhead, and my voice trembled.

Byrone's face relaxed subtly. "You should have died," he said, "but we can rectify that." The gun was out of his pocket before any of us could react. "You are armed, I think, Lastings. Do put your hands up very carefully." He moved, with a peculiar slithery action, around my uncle and slipped a hand into his shoulder holster for the Webley. Then he stepped back and motioned for me to move next to Uncle Lastings. He kept the gun on us.

"Sorry, lad." My uncle put a consoling arm around me. Byrone jerked his head in warning, and Uncle Lastings released me but not before he'd slipped the knife from my pocket. I froze, hardly daring to breathe, but he must somehow have gotten the weapon into his sleeve, because there was no clatter of metal on the floor and no reaction from Byrone, either. My uncle stepped aside, seemingly focused on Alexi, who had gotten to his feet and was impatiently demanding to have his handcuffs removed.

Byrone had a different idea and asked a question. Alexi shook his head and quite surprisingly answered in English. "Is gone with the Frenchman," he said.

Surely he referred to that ominous Russian pistol.

"That's unfortunate," said Byrone. "But I can improvise."

Alexi lurched toward him. Byrone took a step back, gesturing with the Webley, and had him move to the other side of the room. My uncle cleared his throat. "Even if you have prevented Horace from coming, the gendarmes are expected. They will not take kindly to an assault on a respectable family. You and Alexi should clear out now."

Alexi said something in Russian, doubtless in support of this idea.

Byrone shook his silver head. It really belonged on a portrait bust somewhere or on a nice high-denomination coin. "The operation has been successfully concluded. All that remains now is to remove the evidence. You should not have interfered, Lastings."

He raised the pistol.

"If you shoot us, Horace will certainly be suspicious," my uncle said. I noticed that he had moved another step away from me.

"But all the witnesses will be gone. Our little trap has disappeared, leaving a handful of compromised attachés and diplomats, who will be most useful. I will, of course, be investigating the sad case of two British subjects murdered by a Soviet agent."

"Using a British sidearm?" my uncle asked. He'd moved another step away so that he, Alexi, and I were in a rough triangle.

Alexi became agitated. He moved toward the door, doubtless counting on the idea that a man shot in the back would hardly be a good murder suspect. Byrone shouted a warning, and when it was ignored, he reached for Alexi's handcuffs to turn him around. Focused on the Russian, he lowered the revolver for an instant, and I grabbed his wrist.

The revolver discharged with such a tremendous blast that I fell on the floor, a good thing, too, because my uncle leaped over me to send Pavel's knife into Byrone's ribs. A scream and the thump of their bodies before they landed on the floor. They struggled over the Webley until Alexi kicked Byrone in the head with all his strength, lost his balance, and toppled onto the others. The revolver discharged once more, the bullet ricocheting off the base of the oil lamp before an odd silence, broken only by gasps and groans.

My uncle sat up, followed by Alexi, who got to his knees and swung his legs around so that he could lean against the doorjamb. He was quite white and his eyes seemed imperfectly focused. Uncle Lastings had blood on his hands and also on his face from a nasty groove where a bullet had plowed across his cheek. Byrone did not get up, though his chest was heaving. There was enough blood about to make me feel rather sick, and I did not see how he could survive.

I looked at my uncle, who shrugged. "He dies for sure if we remove the knife."

"Let me go," said Alexi. "I can be gone and no questions."

My uncle hesitated. I know by now that nothing is ever simple with him, there are always angles within angles, and I do not know what he would have decided if we had not heard a large vehicle pulling up the drive. I looked out the window. "The gendarmes," I said.

Uncle Lasting shook his head with what might have been regret but might have been satisfaction, too—Alexi, after all, had tried to kill him. "Too late now," he said.

CHAPTER SIXTEEN

The gendarmes arrived, three earnest men with short hair, snappy uniforms, and a preemptory manner that hid neither their youth nor inexperience. Uncle Lastings spotted this right off and put on his best colonel of the regiment voice. "This," he said, pointing to Alexi, "is the man who attacked Madeline Dumoulin and her son, Luc. He is a Russian agent. And this is a British intelligence officer. They will both be of interest to the British embassy and the Deuxième Bureau. I trust you liaise with both."

The gendarme officer looked around the room, took in the pool of blood, Alexi's handcuffs, my costume, and the general disorder. "And who might you be?"

My uncle gave our names and identified us as "friends and acquaintances of Madame Dumoulin, whom we found bound and beaten."

I give the officer credit. If his men looked flummoxed, he recovered enough to observe, "You made an early visit."

"We had reason to be concerned about her welfare," Uncle

Lastings said smoothly. "But this man needs medical attention. He's been stabbed."

"By whom?"

"By me," said Uncle Lastings. "Before he could shoot the three of us. That's his Webley on the floor. My own sidearm is somewhere about his person."

Well, talk about a hullabaloo. The gendarmes had a Russian national who was denying everything and pretending not to speak a word of French. They had my uncle, who'd confessed to grievous bodily harm. They had Stephen Byrone, a British spy, who was probably dying. And they had me, clearly foreign but dressed as a French janitor and looking as if I'd had a run through the sewers.

My uncle wanted them to contact the Deuxième Bureau and our embassy *tout de suite*. When they balked at this, he clammed up about the situation, but he did add that as I was underage, the embassy should be notified. I have to admit that he was eloquent on my behalf. He subtracted three years and a whole lot of experience from his favorite nephew, and if he hadn't been interrupted, I think I'd have come off as a male version of Little Nell.

But the gendarmes realized Byrone's condition was beyond their first aid skills, and after a few frantic minutes, we were all loaded into the van, Alexi still handcuffed. In deference to my supposed age and innocence, I was put in front beside the driver. The officer and the second gendarme sat in the back with my uncle, Alexi, and Byrone, who after a jolting ride over the country roads, was delivered to the nearest hospital more or less dead. I didn't feel too chipper myself.

I didn't improve until late in the day, when I was plucked from the gendarmerie by an embassy official. I'd spent most of the time in a locked room, one step up from a cell, with a cup of coffee and a baguette for company. I put my arms on the table and my head on my arms and fell asleep. At one point, the officer who had picked us up visited me. I declined to answer further questions without someone from the embassy, claiming that my French was inadequate. That was actually true, but I'm not sure my English would have unraveled the whole thing, either.

Finally, late in the afternoon, salvation appeared in the shape of Willington, my nostalgic friend from the reception at the embassy. The door opened, and in he came, blond and handsome, complete with attaché case, striped suit, and an air of effortless perfection. I was to be released. That was excellent. Into his custody. That might or might not be good.

"Where's Uncle Horace?" I asked. It was quite possible that I was no longer his nephew, but he still should have answered my real uncle's call for help.

Willington cleared his throat and looked as uncomfortable as a well-trained diplomat could. "Horace has been taken ill," he said.

Illness covers a multitude of sins. "Was he drinking?"

"Really!" said Willington. He had haughty indignation down to perfection.

"I'm here because I was drugged with a glass of wine."

He gave me a look. "Horace has been known to take a drink, but we hadn't considered that."

"Better consider it now. And where's Lastings? Is he all right?"

"He's being questioned. We have someone with him. But you have been released." He frowned. "We'll need to get you cleaned up."

I was about to tell him that all my clothes were at Lastings's flat when I caught myself. Horace, for whatever reason, was out of commission. Uncle Lastings was being questioned. Alexi, I guessed, was awaiting a Russian translator, and Pavel was, for the moment, safely out of the way. Unless Chaput's lost photographs were retrieved, there would be no proof that any of the embassy staff had been compromised by visiting the house on the rue Jacob. So unless Alexi talked or Pavel reappeared, I had no idea whom to trust.

I decided to insist on "Uncle" Horace and demanded he be informed immediately. "He'll want to know where I am." I imagined a concerned parent and added, "Mother will be frightfully angry with him about this. I think you'd better take me straight to the embassy."

We were in the car by this time, and he sniffed and said I needed a change of clothes first. Where might mine be?

"Lost," I said. "All quite ruined. Hence the coveralls."

He wanted to know where I'd gotten them.

"I stole them. Needs must," I said, sounding alarmingly like Uncle Lastings. I hadn't realized how deception affects one's speech. But I declined to tell him about the rue Jacob or the tunnel or anything else until I had some idea of what he knew and what he was up to.

"I might have something that would do you for the moment," he said, and when we reached the city, he set his

course not for the embassy, but for a building near Uncle Lastings's flat. Willington had a top-floor apartment, just as spiffy
and correct as his dress, and he had me leave my shoes and the
coveralls at the door.

I agreed that I could do with a bath but, remembering the
notorious Brides in the Bath case, I locked the door. There was
plenty of hot water. Marvelous. I watched the mud and scum of
the tunnel spiral down the drain and got out and wrapped myself
in a good Turkish towel. In some ways, I believe I could live like
a diplomat.

Willington was waiting with underwear, a pair of slacks—
clean but far too big—and a shirt—ditto. Prefects and rugby
forwards come large. I dressed under his watchful—lecherous?—
eye and announced my eagerness to see Uncle Horace.

Willington sat down and took a sip from a large glass of whiskey. "Horace Caruthers is not your uncle."

I resorted to the Gallic shrug. "In a manner of speaking," I
said. "He and mother are related somehow."

Willington shook his head. "My best guess is that you are one
of Lastings's bum boys." He added a gimlet-eyed look of disapproval. "Introduced to embassy personnel for unknown reasons."

I sat down and said nothing.

"Horace, as I've explained, is out of commission."

"I can wait," I said.

He sampled his drink again. "If released onto the street, you
might be vulnerable." He turned his wrist to check his watch.
"Possibly you have no lodgings at the moment. Possibly you
have enemies."

"Possibly I can take care of myself." I hoped I sounded confident and fearless. Willington no longer struck me as the golden prefect and rugby star but as the house bully who liked to wake smaller boys in the middle of the night for some humiliating prank.

"Look, we're on the same side," he said, sounding a more conciliatory note and pouring me a drink. "With Horace out of action, I've been charged with wrapping up the loose ends. We have a chat, you tell me what you know, I put you on the boat train. How would that be?"

I shook my head. "My passport is pretty much ruined."

He flapped one hand. "That can be managed. I can see you have documents."

"Too bad I don't have any information for you."

Willington sat very still. I could see the white of his knuckles as he gripped the whiskey glass. "The man you were arrested with, the Russian, was he known to you?"

"Not well."

"But you did know him."

"I knew who he was but not what he was up to."

"Someone said there might be another boy involved."

I tried to look blank.

"A Russian boy?"

I kept quiet.

"A boy you were looking for? You and Lastings?"

When I remained silent, Willington snatched at the front of my shirt and with his face inches from mine shouted, "Is he dead?"

"He was caught in the explosion."

Willington stared at me, his chilly eyes unblinking, but I'm a good liar, and, in fact, both Pavel and I *had* been caught in the blast.

"But you know about him," he said, releasing me and sitting back down. Was that a note of regret? Had he been susceptible to my charm after all? "You're the only witness."

I felt a little chill: I had not been quite as clever as I'd thought. While my uncle, Pavel, and Alexi all could provide evidence about the honeypot scheme, I'd foolishly let Willington think I was the only one besides Alexi who'd had contact with Pavel. Alexi might well keep quiet for the glory of the revolution and the advancement of the Soviets, but I was a problem, whether Willington was set to betray our country or just aiming to escape the threat of blackmail. *Keep alert, Francis!*

"I believe I need a lawyer. I want to see Horace and I want to see Lastings, who really is my uncle. You can check on that." Good enough? I took a sip of the whiskey. Excellent. And then another before caution took over. I set the glass down still more than half full.

"Perhaps you're right. Drink up and we'll go to the embassy," he said. "Horace should have sobered up by now." I got a toothy smile; in addition to everything else, he had perfect teeth.

"Enough for me. I've hardly had anything to eat today." Cue for him to offer a snack to a growing boy. Instead, he lunged at me, trapping my legs and grabbing my jaw. He snatched the whiskey glass and put it to my lips. "Drink up," he said.

I shook my head and tried to twist away, but he was too strong. He got a certain amount down my throat; the rest drenched my shirt. Willington hoisted me to my feet, twisted one arm behind me and forced me to the door. "Yell," he said, "and I'll break your arm."

With this caution, we descended the stair. *One good kick*, I thought to myself. A strategic elbow. Maybe even a deliberate fall—although the stone steps of the lower floors looked uninviting, and between drugs and little sleep and less food I was feeling wobbly. Still, how hard could it be? I grabbed the banister, intending to hang on, and found my feet knocked out from under me. *Bump, bump, bump* down on my shins, upright again at the door and quick out to the car and in.

Door locked behind me. I tried to clamber over to the driver's-side door, but Willington was agile despite his size, and he didn't fool about. I saw his arm go back before his fist hit my face full force. I was thrown against the door frame, where I must have cracked my head, because the next thing I was aware of was motion passing through alternating darkness and brightness. The car was moving fast, disturbing my twitching stomach, and I struggled to sit up.

Silhouettes of trees against the night sky—we were in some sylvan place, not the embassy. Not safety. Not safe. And now a glimmer. Lights, of course, it was night, full dark. Darkness had come while I was foolishly lying to Willington and making myself seem dangerous. But that was a glimmer and a reflection. So water. The river. We were along the Seine and why were we there? No good reason, no good reason at all. Were we slowing?

For one of the quays? So convenient for the romantic and the suicidal and the romantically suicidal.

I wanted to tell Willington that I was a survivor. That romance was not in my portfolio. That, moreover, my distaste for deep water was well known, but I couldn't find the words. Not in French, but Willington was not French, he was English. English words then. Easy, sure, unless your tongue was paralyzed. Was I paralyzed? I moved one hand. Not paralyzed.

I put it on the door. Felt the door handle. Felt the lock. Saw against the blurry outlines of chestnut trees and the glimmer of the streetlights, figures. Friends? Enemies? *Better than Willington*, I thought, and pushed down with my remaining strength. The door swung open, carrying me out with it. My feet hit the cobblestones at alarming speed. Willington yelled and the brakes screeched as I hit the road, slid over the cobbles, and crashed into the curbing in terrible pain.

I screamed. Then high, alarmed shouts and a clatter of women's heels was followed by the most beautiful sound in the world. "Hoy, ducks! Good way to kill yourself!"

The voice belonged to a big blonde with a fine London accent.

"Help! He's trying to kill me! Car. Man in car."

An earsplitting whistle. Her partner, a leggy brunette with a strong line in perfume, grabbed me under the arms and hauled me from the road onto the sidewalk and under the trees. Willington shouted at them, but they were tough and not easily frightened. The blonde yelled back at him in the finest French slang, and I can't guess what might have happened to him or to my two Amazons if another dark car hadn't screeched to a stop. Two men got out.

"Shite! First gents of the night and we've a casualty on our hands," one of the women said.

I looked up, recognized my two uncles, and passed out.

Hospital room. Mine. I was sitting up, all clean and bright, my left arm encased in what felt like a ton of plaster, my cut head decorated with patches. More bandages covered the raw scrapes on hip, shoulder, and side from my excursion along the cobblestones. I had a severe break, a possible concussion, and contusions, which sound more medically impressive than bruises.

Nonetheless, I was up and eating well—check my chart if you don't believe me—and ready to be released. At that moment, I was enjoying late strawberries from a basket that Madame Dumoulin had brought me, along with a stack of gallery catalogs. Both were immensely welcome, as was the news that everyone was safe and that with only tinted glasses and a little makeup, Madame Dumoulin had been out and about, without, as she put it, *looking a spectacle*, and had seen a most interesting show by a Japanese painter.

That was on Thursday, her day for Paris, and I immediately felt better than I had since before I ventured into Willington's apartment. But now it was Saturday, and, sure enough, right at 1100 hours, in came Uncle Lastings. He was wearing a dark, ultrarespectable suit, and he was carrying a neat little attaché case. That had to mean something.

He reached into the basket and helped himself to a couple of berries. "Very nice."

"From Madame Dumoulin."

He shook his head. "A charming widow. You might have introduced me, Francis. You might have made your old uncle's fortune."

"And she might have lost hers. She is a good friend," I said.

He made a face. "So I understand. For some mysterious reason, you bring out the protective instinct in women, a gift of the gods you choose to neglect. The two flappers the other night—"

"Probably saved my life. I hope they didn't lose by it."

"Lose by it? Dear boy, I took them to dinner and rogered them both. A charming night!"

Did I believe that he would have left his unconscious nephew to romp with the Amazons? Actually, I did.

"Horace, of course, arranged everything at this end. A private room and the very best of everything."

"I appreciate. And Pavel?"

"Safe as houses. He's given a very complete statement, and his papers are all arranged. He and Jules and the beautiful Inessa are off to Canada for a time." He looked at his watch. "They catch the boat train to England today, then on to Montreal. Best to have them well away from Paris."

"That's good," I said, and I leaned my head back on my chair, suddenly tired. My friends had been much on my mind.

"Well," said my uncle, "that's that, then." He clapped his hands and made to rise.

"You're forgetting my money," I said. "Twenty-five pounds."

He huffed and he puffed about this. There had been unexpected costs. My hospital stay, clothes, et cetera.

"I need twenty-five pounds," I said, "or I go to the press:

BRITISH BOY ENDANGERED AS EMBASSY BUNGLES HONEYPOT INVESTIGATION. How does that sound?"

Well, my uncle got angry before he turned sly; he was a man who always had an alternate plan of attack. He lit one of his Gauloises, looked up at the ceiling, then back at me with a twinkle in his eye. "You really are going to set up in London as a designer?"

"Yes. With Nan."

"She's found a place for you?"

"She has. Bedroom, kitchen, WC, and workroom/showroom. I can do it."

"There would be storage space?"

"Some. As I get more stock, I'll have to expand. But, yes, if Nan says the place will do, you can be sure it will."

"Give me the address," he said. And when I did, he opened his wallet and took out some five- and ten-pound notes. "I might just ship you something."

I had a pretty good idea of what that might be, and I didn't much like getting involved with his art scam. At the same time, the chance to study a Matisse, a Derain, or a Marquet up close and at my leisure was almost irresistible. "There will be storage fees," I said, "and you'll have to pay the insurance."

Uncle Lastings looked at me from under his brows and considered being angry again but decided against it. "I didn't take you for a man of business, Francis. I hope this hardheaded streak does not interfere with your artistic inclinations." Then he laughed and asked, "Any other requirements?"

I stood up, a trifle uncertainly but, yes, I was on my feet, and yes, I was going home. "Only a telegram to Nan," I said. "Tell her to meet me at the boat train at Victoria Station."

ABOUT THE AUTHOR

Janice Law is an acclaimed author of mystery fiction. The Watergate scandal inspired her to write her first novel, *The Big Payoff,* which introduced Anna Peters, a street-smart young woman who blackmails her boss, a corrupt oil executive. The novel was a success, winning an Edgar nomination, and Law went on to write eight more in the series. Law has written historical mysteries, standalone suspense, and, most recently, the Francis Bacon Mysteries, which include *The Prisoner of the Riviera,* winner of the 2013 Lambda Literary Gay Mystery Award. She lives and writes in Connecticut.

THE FRANCIS BACON MYSTERIES

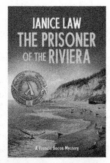

MYSTERIOUSPRESS.COM

Otto Penzler, owner of the Mysterious Bookshop in Manhattan, founded the Mysterious Press in 1975. Penzler quickly became known for his outstanding selection of mystery, crime, and suspense books, both from his imprint and in his store. The imprint was devoted to printing the best books in these genres, using fine paper and top dust-jacket artists, as well as offering many limited, signed editions.

Now the Mysterious Press has gone digital, publishing ebooks through **MysteriousPress.com**.

MysteriousPress.com offers readers essential noir and suspense fiction, hard-boiled crime novels, and the latest thrillers from both debut authors and mystery masters. Discover classics and new voices, all from one legendary source.

THE MYSTERIOUS BOOKSHOP, founded in 1979, is located in Manhattan's Tribeca neighborhood. It is the oldest and largest mystery-specialty bookstore in America.

The shop stocks the finest selection of new mystery hardcovers, paperbacks, and periodicals. It also features a superb collection of signed modern first editions, rare and collectable works, and Sherlock Holmes titles. The bookshop issues a free monthly newsletter highlighting its book clubs, new releases, events, and recently acquired books.

58 Warren Street
info@mysteriousbookshop.com
(212) 587-1011
Monday through Saturday
11:00 a.m. to 7:00 p.m.

FIND OUT MORE AT:

www.mysteriousbookshop.com

FOLLOW US:

@TheMysterious and Facebook.com/MysteriousBookshop

OPEN ROAD

INTEGRATED MEDIA

Find a full list of our authors and
titles at www.openroadmedia.com

FOLLOW US
@OpenRoadMedia

CPSIA information can be obtained
at www.ICGtesting.com
Printed in the USA
BVOW08s2020250117
474400BV00005B/4/P